BUNKHOUSE SHOWDOWN

Keogh idly shuffled the cards again and laid them on the table without looking away from Dant. If he was going to take Dant's place as foreman, Keogh had to best him in front of the crew.

The tension showed plainly on the men. Though none of them had made so much as an open move during all this palaver, Keogh observed the stiffness of their bodies and the morose, brooding watchfulness of their faces. Cool and thoughtful, he considered this outfit. They had him blocked, there was no back door and not much room to shift on one side or another. Yet that was as much of an advantage as it was a disadvantage, for if a play came up he was cleared for action and they were badly crowded. Any bullet of his would reach one of them.

Dant's lips had come together in a long, bloodless line and Keogh knew for a certainty the current foreman was traveling along a similar line of reasoning.

And it suddenly became a matter of nerves. . . .

ERNEST HAYCOX

SIXGUN DUO

PINNACLE BOOKS
WINDSOR PUBLISHING CORP.

PINNACLE BOOKS

are published by

Windsor Publishing Corp.
475 Park Avenue South
New York, NY 10016

First Pinnacle Books printing: September, 1990

Printed in the United States of America

The Gun Singer

Chapter One

All morning that faint ball of dust kept behind Bill Keogh and his claybank as he pressed across the barren Horn Peak Desert, but around four o'clock the telltale signal shifted, raced abreast on the far right and finally disappeared in the foreground. Keogh's lids narrowed against the brassy heat-haze westward and guessed the maneuver; the following man apparently had figured out which way he, Keogh, was going and intended to get there first. So when at six of a burning day Keogh crossed the treeless square of King's Plaza and reined up at a saloon, he was prepared for grief.

He had been prepared for grief ever since entering the Horn Peak twenty-four hours previously. This land—isolated, unfriendly—was perpetually roiled with the intrigues of factions. Moreover, Bill Keogh was a lone rider of that lank and rawboned breed which seemed always to attract the wheeling buzzards of ill-omen. Thus he was keyed for the unexpected. The rugged, deeply-bronzed cheeks were grave and a sharp gleam broke through the deceptive slumber of his violet-gray eyes. In one swift and sweeping glance he saw all he needed to see, the alkaline desolation of this three-sided town, the dark visages staring at him from shadowed recesses, and the man with bitten features who stood at the saloon rack and fiddled with the reins of a dust-caked piebald. It was mighty plain that the piebald had just finished a hard run.

The showdown was right here, and he knew it. But he scarcely expected it to come about so abruptly. As he dismounted and wheeled toward the saloon door, the piebald's owner moved across his pathway with a swaggering carelessness that made the whole play crystal clear to Keogh. He could have prevented the collision by a sudden wrench of his body but a flash of cool wisdom told him he would only be delaying inevitable conflict. Nor was Keogh a man given to meekness. If this fellow wanted it, he could have it, and so he kept his stride. The impact was slanting, severe. Keogh's hundred-eighty pounds boomed against the other's flank, turned him completely around in a staggering circle and dashed him against the saloon wall. Keogh stopped short, soberly waiting.

"Damnation!" said the fellow in a harsh, scolding voice, "look where you're goin'!"

He had small, brilliant eyes set very narrow on either side of an extremely sharp nose. When he drew his lips back to let out the angry hostile words, Keogh saw a mouth bare of teeth except for two side teeth; it gave him a wolfish look. The anger seemed half real, half arranged. Keogh, still waiting out the play, kept silent.

8

"Pilgrims like you got no business shoulderin' around the Plaza high an' cocky," growled the fellow. Then, having said this, he paused, measuring Keogh with a calculating glance. What he found apparently encouraged him, for his manner turned rougher. "Look here, you slab-sided galoot, I got a notion to rub the paint offen you!"

"Never check a notion," said Keogh. "It might stunt your growth. If you got a good idea, go to it."

Slight surprise appeared on the narrow face of the other. "What's that?"

"You heard me," grunted Keogh. "Your manner is lousy and your way of drumming up trouble is raw. Apparently you left school halfway through the kindergarten grade. Nobody could be so dumb as to make a sashay like this and figure the other man wasn't wise to it. You been on my trail all day. Here I am—what of it?"

The surprise spread across the other's sullen cheeks. "How'd you know that?"

"I picked up the color of that piebald with my field glasses early this mornin'," stated Keogh, and turned suddenly severe. "Spit it out. What's botherin' you?"

The counterattack threw the fellow off stride. Defensively he ceased to talk and the bluff brutality of his manner shifted to a shrewd and increasing watchfulness. Keogh stood there reading the transformation on the other's thin, vulpine face. This man was more dangerous than he had at first estimated—more dangerous because he had the power to shift his mind under fire. The beaded brilliancy of his close eyes increased as he broke the silence.

9

"Don't get up on your ear, pilgrim," he grunted. "I followed you because I wanted to know what a strange stray was up to. We're particular in this country."

"Hokum," snapped Bill Keogh. "Plain hokum. But you started something. Now what do you propose to do about it?"

The fellow's head turned toward the saloon and snapped back, lip and mouth thinning. Keogh recognized a cold courage in the man, but he saw also that something checked the impulse to move into action. Whatever the restraining impulse was, it had sufficient force to turn the man and move him down the street. Keogh walked through the saloon doors.

Before he had reached the bar he clearly understood he was in the cross-rip of a deeply troubled tide. The saloon was full of silent loungers, all standing with faces toward the door and in attitudes of expectancy. Coming abreast the bar he concluded he was suspected of packing a star, or if not that, then of being an imported trigger twister. Such things happened in country like this. And he'd been under suspicion before.

"Straight with a chaser," said he to the bartender.

But it wasn't the bartender who served him. Another man cruised out of the crowd, walked behind the bar and set up a bottle and a glass. He was ponderous, this individual, and the heat added on an oily sweat to his features. He had an indoor color, loose jowls making a cowling within which all the rest of his facial marks lay flattened like those of a bulldog. Resting both arms on the mahogany, he stared closely at Bill Keogh.

10

"So you braced Sam Veen?" he said in a queer, flute-like tenor.

"Veen's his handle?" parried Keogh, measuring his drink into the glass. "Well, I don't think so high of somebody's judgment."

The big man's eyes narrowed. "As how?"

"Whoever sicced Veen on my trail," pursued Keogh casually, conscious that the whole saloon listened in, "forgot to give him orders enough. Veen finds I don't wilt like he figured. He ain't sure what to do next. Don't you reckon now he'll have to go back for further instructions?"

"To who?" muttered the big man.

"I'd like to know," admitted Keogh, and downed his whiskey. "Maybe you could tell me."

"Not me, brother. I'm Lake Shadders and all I do is run a saloon. Speakin' as a friend to all mankind, don't be too wrong about Veen. I've seen others make the same fatal error. Did you say you come from the county seat?"

Some pair in the back of the saloon fell to a violent quarreling and Shadders stared in that direction, still and cold. The quarreling halted instantly, whereupon Bill Keogh laid that token of Shadders' authority away in his mind. There was an increasing strain in the place; the crowd, he found, watched Shadders closely. On the point of replying, he was diverted by the entry of another man whose straight body and square shoulders were braced defiantly toward the onlookers. His hair was gray at the temples, his mouth bitter around the corners. Keogh, placing him as a ranchowner type, heard Shadders speak with a mock deference.

11

"Honored by your presence, Mister Tallen. What can I do for you?"

Tallen never bothered to reply. Walking to the tobacco case, he took a handful of cigars and flung a dollar down; the ringing echo of it was startling in the packed silence. Keogh's brain ran rapidly and his senses swelled to catch the undercurrent of hatred and treachery playing through the saloon. This Tallen's appearance had a freezing effect, but for his own part he bit off the end of a cigar indifferently and applied a match. Over the tip of flame, Keogh caught the direct impact of level, scrutinizing eyes. Still silently imperturbable, Tallen measured him without secrecy or apology. Lake Shadders spoke again, bearing more heavily on the words.

"Think you can use him, Tallen?"

Tallen flung up his head, saying angrily, "If I'm any judge of an honest man, Shadders, you can't use him!"

"So—" grunted Shadders, and bit off the rest of the remark. The doors swung again, this time violently. Sam Veen came in, his wolfish visage contorted by anger. Placing Keogh, Veen turned, body swinging forward, both elbows crooked and his palms flattened toward his thighs. It was too clear a signal to miss and Keogh gently pushed himself away from the bar.

"I'll argue the point with you some farther," growled Veen.

"I see you got more instructions," drawled Keogh. "What's it to be?"

"To hell with your line of talk," snapped Veen. "You said some things to me I won't stand for."

"You stood for them a minute ago," observed

Keogh. "Did you walk around town to work up a good mad spell?"

"Eat that, brother!" cried Veen. "Eat it!"

The sun had gone down and a clouded blue twilight swirled through the saloon. As if moved by a common force, the idling loungers moved away, against the walls. Keogh, slim and rigid, saw Veen's eyes burning and glittering. It was not a new situation for Keogh, but one coldly remote cell of his mind balanced the chances and found them uneven. He was no fire-eater. In his time, he had backed down, playing for a better deal. During the course of his twenty-six years he had mastered strategy, had discovered that a soft word and a seeming lack of courage sometimes performed more marvels than the smash of a bullet. But now, the long pursuing grief arrived and not to be evaded, he figured a soft word to be of no avail. King's Plaza was a cold deck town. There never would be a better deal.

"Supposin' I don't?" he murmured.

"You—" bawled Veen, adding an unmistakable word.

Bill Keogh's body turned to woven wire. One moment he stood idle by the bar; the next moment he was half across the separating interval. Sam Veen's gun arm dropped, his body broke away from the charging Keogh. But before he could draw, Keogh's hundred-eighty pounds exploded against him, carried him all the way back to the saloon wall, smashed him against it with a force that capsized a bracket lamp and sent it jangling to the floor. Veen ripped his revolver clear, rolled and tried to bring it into play, in answer to which Keogh's left forearm dropped like

13

an ax across the other's wrist. Veen yelled, the gun dropped. Keogh's strong arms caught Veen at the hips, lifted him and flung him across a poker table.

It would have broken the man's back if the table had not tipped and sent Veen sliding head first into a corner. Veen yelled again, shaken with rage. He pulled himself up and lashed out at the advancing Keogh with both fists. Keogh, forgetting all caution and all need of guard, felt those blows sink into his stomach, jar the regular beating of his heart. Then he had Veen around the waist again. The doors were directly ahead of him. Lifting Veen, snapping Veen's spine with one enormous constriction of arm, he threw the man into those doors. Veen went through with a strangled oath, stumbled on the steps and rolled across the sidewalk. Keogh followed, but some leaping black devil in his mind changed his thoughts for a brief, devastating moment; he caught hold of one of the doors and bore down on it until the hinges screamed free of the dry wood; he flung the door into the saloon behind him.

Veen had absorbed the punishment and risen. Out of instinct he clawed at his belt, found the gun missing and elected to charge. Keogh's turning hip caught the full effect of that attack and one stunning, mauling blow set off crimson lights in his head. He reached for Veen. The latter, twice bruised by those bear-like hugs, teetered on his heels and retreated. Keogh's head dropped, and he rushed Veen, tore aside the latter's weaving fists and dropped the troublemaker with an upswinging smash that sounded as if it had splintered all the teeth Veen had left. The man went down soundlessly, rolled once

14

and lay senseless.

Keogh bent over, unhooked Veen's gunbelt and flung it behind him. When he turned he saw all the saloon loungers grouped on the walk and Lake Shadders standing massively silent. He saw all this through a film of fighting anger that died reluctantly from his vision. Poised in his tracks, he watched Lake Shadders, more and more convinced the gross saloonman held the answer to this affair behind those inscrutable eyes.

"When you do a job," muttered Shadders, thoughtfully, "you sure do it complete."

"Tell this Veen," said Keogh coldly, "when he wakes up, to go get some more instructions."

"He'll be seein' you again soon," replied Shadders. "I'm tellin' you not to mistake him."

"You mean," countered Keogh, "that he'll be sent against me again."

"Have it like you please."

Keogh turned and crossed the square toward a hotel whose lights made a winking row through the deepening shadows. Now that the swift, destroying impulses had quieted, he was outraged at himself. "Damn a man that goes hogwild like I do," he grunted. "I lay myself wide open and one of these days I'll get laid out because of it."

He went up the hotel porch and inside to an empty dining room. Eating in solitary gloom, his mind kept jabbing at the corners of the mystery he was plunged into. But the ready answer wouldn't come and the usual explanations didn't seem to fit. He laid a half dollar on the table and walked back to the porch. Tapering a cigarette, and staring across to the

15

saloon, he became suddenly aware of a figure sitting alone in the deepest dark of the porch. This figure shifted, spoke quietly.

"Yonder to the east you can see the outline of the Horn Peak hills. Make a pretty line against the dark, don't they?"

It sounded like Tallen's voice—the fellow he had pegged as a cattleman. "Yeah," mused Keogh.

"Only eighteen miles across the desert to those hills," pursued Tallen. "Eighteen short miles. You'd think it easy to make the distance in a couple hours, wouldn't you?"

Keogh kept quiet, knowing Tallen was working toward a subject. Tallen shifted and swore quietly. "But it ain't, my boy. Almost impossible to get there. I been a week trying it and I ain't got no farther than the edge of this town. I observe you're some handy at fightin'."

"Not proud of it," muttered Keogh.

"You better be," said Tallen moodily. "You better be damned proud of it. Listen to me." His voice dropped to a soft murmur. "In my pocket is a letter. It should go to a fellow named Henry LaTouche over in those hills. Over in a settlement crowded at the bottom of that gash you can just make out against the skyline. One hundred dollars to you, my boy, if you take the letter and deliver it."

"And then what?" questioned Keogh, not greatly interested.

"Unnecessary question," said Tallen. "All you got to do is get there. A hundred dollars. Fifty of it now."

"I don't know," reflected Keogh, still watching the saloon. "The boys around here have put the pinchers

16

on me. I'm sort of interested in figuring it out. Not in a hurry to retreat."

A long silence ensued, broken at last by Tallen. "As for that, don't worry. You'll meet them all again, here or in the hills. But I won't urge it. Thought you was another kind of a scrapper."

Keogh, shrewd and easy-going as he was, lived by impulse. To want to do a thing was ample excuse for going ahead and Tallen's last phrase somehow changed the whole current of his thoughts. For one brief moment he visualized Tallen's face as he had seen it in the saloon—a weary and bitter face. An honest face turned without hope against Lake Shadders.

"All right," said Keogh. "I'm your cookie."

Tallen rose and a long sigh came out of him. "Good—mighty good. I didn't have a card in my hand till you came along. You're my last bet, boy."

He walked toward Keogh slowly. He walked up to Keogh and past him, but in going by he slid a wadded fold of paper into Keogh's hands. Never stopping, he descended the hotel steps and aimed across the square, quiet words coming back. "There's the letter and the fifty. Henry LaTouche, at Last Chance, across the desert and up that gash in the hills. And listen—don't figure the job done until you personally face LaTouche. That ought to be warnin' enough."

"Look here," called Keogh. "What's next with you?"

The answer was small and short. "To die, I guess."

Keogh stood fast a little while, watching Tallen drift into darkness. The man's talk of death was like a gunshot and it roused Keogh's senses again to hard

17

alertness. For the first time he scanned the area to either side of the porch where great pools of black lay thick and dark. Nothing stirred in them and the sidewalk was without an occupant. Yet this very fact reacted immediately on Keogh's questing mind; slipping the letter and the money into a pocket, he left the porch and went over the square. Coming beside his horse, he turned to look around. A man moved slowly across the hotel porch and joined another who stepped from the bright rectangle of the door.

"Sure," muttered Keogh. "I'd be a sucker to think they wasn't listenin' in. Now—"

He wasn't going to get out so easy, that was mighty plain. Tallen's words became more important as he recollected them—never consider this job done until he actually faced Henry LaTouche. Reaching for the racked reins, he swept the sidewalk along the south line of King's Plaza. Three buildings to the left of the saloon was the wide, dark mouth of a stable, one man loitering there indolently. Of a sudden—as if his act of taking the reins had produced all this—other lounging figures broke out of the obscure angles and alleyways roundabout. There was one posted in the middle of the square, apparently lying on the ground until now; and to his right hand somebody stirred on another dark porch and lit a match. The saloon doors opened, a half-drunk rolling through and halting so as to keep those doors from swinging shut. Thus caught squarely in the light, Keogh made up his mind. Instead of swinging to the saddle, he led the horse toward the stable.

"Not leavin'?"

18

Until now he hadn't seen Lake Shadders. But it was Lake Shadders' voice that challenged him, and Lake Shadders' beefy body that parted from the general blackness adjoining the saloon and crossed the sidewalk. Keogh paused.

"Come along," said he, casual and sleepy. "I'm stablin' for the evenin'."

Shadders halted, glowing tip of a cigar appearing from a cupped palm. His big head swung forward and his heavy-jowled face became half identified. "I wouldn't want to lose your company so sudden," he muttered. "When I meet a fighter I like to make propositions to him."

"What kind?"

Shadders evaded the question. "It's a great country for fighters, son. Providin' they're on the right side o' the chalk line. I'm just mentionin' that to you. Like to give all the boys such friendly advice as I can."

"Come along while I put up the pony," urged Keogh.

Shadders looked to either side of him swiftly. "I'll wait here till you come back."

"It'll be just a minute or so," said Keogh, and walked on. He turned into the stable mouth, met a rising shadow.

"Hostler," drawled Keogh, "I'll need a brush and a currycomb. Bring a lantern, will you?"

He led the claybank on down the runway, the shadow doggedly keeping abreast of him and saying morosely, "That stall—hold on—that stall."

Keogh reached the back end before halting. He flipped the reins up to the saddle horn, walked slowly around until the hostler was against him, an

19

unyielding body.

"How about that lantern, hostler?"

"Yonder," said the hostler. "You go get it."

"Well, if I got to," muttered Keogh and swung all the weight of his right shoulder into a cutting blow that struck the hostler under the flat of his chin and dropped him without a sigh. Yet as quickly and as quietly as it was done, the telegraph of trouble began to send out its messages. Keogh sprang about the horse, made the saddle at one jump and heard a high voice yelling into the stable. "Hold on there! Gentry—block that duffer!" And over and above it came Lake Shadders' tenor shout.

"Get him! Out here, boys! Blast your hides, out here! Tallen—watch Tallen there!"

Keogh tarried one more moment, for Tallen was inside the stable now, and crying his last stand to the forces enveloping him. "Go on, my boy! Go on! Shadders, may God everlastingly damn you, I'm playin' my last card! Go on, boy! They won't get past me in a hurry!"

Keogh wasted no more time. Sinking his spurs, he flashed through the back stable door into blind blackness and let the claybank have his head. The claybank's feet smashed into loose rubbish, floundered in a mess of loose wire and lunged magnificently clear of it. Back of Keogh was a full and heavy belch of gun roar. Boards snapped where the slugs struck through. Shadders' yell rose to a screaming impatience. Tallen was replying. Tallen's voice followed Keogh, bitter and obstinate. "I'm playin' my last hand, Shadders. I'm—" And then Tallen said nothing more. The blasting guns silenced him and

20

King's Plaza swirled and shuddered with a livelier fire. Keogh raced by a line of sheds, low in the saddle as he passed them. The claybank shied and a purple-crimson flower of muzzle light bloomed in Keogh's face, the breath of the bullet fanning his face. He was beyond the ambusher in a moment and his own replying bullet silenced that lone threat. Ahead of him lay open desert and to the eastward ran the jagged silhouette of the Horn Peak hills. Turning the claybank a little he paced away from King's Plaza. The gun shots diminished and died.

"He died with his boots on and scrappin' back," muttered Keogh, thinking of Tallen. "And here am I, up to my ears in another man's trouble. No way out of it now." Half a mile from town he reined in and instantly heard the deep rumble of a cavalcade in pursuit. Afterwards he pushed the claybank for all the beast was worth.

Chapter Two

Two miles onward Keogh halted again to listen. This time the reverberations of pursuit had died to uncertain faintness; and from the tone of the sound he couldn't tell whether the men of King's Plaza were directly behind him or off on a flank. Once more laying his course dead against the black notch cut out of the eastern skyline, he pushed forward at a slightly reduced pace.

As he rode, he recalled Tallen's words about the dangers of this eighteen-mile trip across the desert. He wondered about that. The desert was large and the pursuing outfit had lost ground in the darkness. If things went along as they were going now, where was the difficulty in reaching the hill settlement around midnight or before?

Having asked himself the question, he tried to answer it by setting up every manner of unforeseen difficulty. The fact that he couldn't see how the pursuers would be able to trap him here in the dark meant nothing. Tallen had said the desert was full of disaster and Tallen had known what he was talking about. So, where was the catch?

"I don't see how they can overhaul me," he reflected. "Only thing is, they might send a fire signal on ahead to warn another bunch in the hills. But I don't see any sign of that. But, wait a minute. They know now I'm on Tallen's business—which means they know I'm bound for that notch. So, if they did manage to cut around and get ahead of me, they'd expect to find me on the direct trail to the notch. Therefore, Mister Keogh, you better loop a little bit."

He was a hand to carry out his convictions immediately. So, having made up his mind, he turned the claybank south of the direct line he now traveled along, and made a long detour through the night. There was danger in this too. The pursuers might hit the settlement while he was occupied out here with dodging. Might hit it and lay for him. Speed, in his case, was about as essential as strategy; and after falling a good three or four miles south of the direct route, he began angling back. A deep, unfathomed pall lay over the flat land, the stars glittered relentlessly without glow, and there was no moon. All sound of Lake Shadders' men was gone.

It was Lake Shadders he was dealing with. There could be no doubt of that after hearing the saloon man's bellowing participation in the affair at King's Plaza. A great deal more had been made clear to Keogh at the same time. There was something in the hills Shadders wanted. And something Tallen wanted. Well, Tallen was dead, but he'd played a last hand well—so well that Shadders was out with all his men.

"I don't know what this is all about," grunted Keogh to the pointed ears of the claybank. "But I'm in it anyhow. That's me all over. I ride into a scope of country, somebody pokes me in the ribs and I get sore. Somebody else offers me a chance to fight back, whereupon I'm the goat for a whole confounded country to shoot at. Strong back, weak mind."

He was driving ahead now with the notch a little on his right cheek. The claybank, always a resolute and willing animal, checked in without warning and Keogh stiffened. He knew better than to push the animal when it so clearly sensed danger. Bending forward, Keogh tried to penetrate the blank, black wall ahead. He saw nothing. But the claybank was swinging around at a walk, going almost at right angles to the former course; and in a little while the horse halted altogether. Keogh stepped to the ground, threw down the reins and walked on cautiously.

The next moment he stopped short on his heels, nose pointed into a chasm. The floor of the desert marched up to a sharp rim and dropped from sight. Apparently the slash was of considerable dimensions and quite deep, for he could see neither the bottom nor the far wall; and when he settled on his stomach, head hooked over the rim, he discovered that the near wall fell straight and bare like the side of a box. In thirty seconds he saw all he wanted to see and was back in the saddle, cursing himself. Turning north and paralleling the rim at an urgent pace, he supplied the answer to his former question.

"Hell, but I'm bright! There's why the trail to the Horn Peaks is so doggone troubled. Probably only

24

one place to cross this canyon and if it ain't guarded now by Shadders' men I'm an angel with gilded wings! So thought I'd be cautious, did I?"

The claybank was tired and was inclined to slack off. Keogh spoke sharply and used the threat of his spur points. The damage was done now. No use crying, no use delaying. Meanwhile the rim of the canyon began to slope, indicating a crossing not far ahead. Half a mile onward the descending contour of the land broke into a series of wrinkles. Keogh brought his pony to a walk and lifted his gun across his lap. Drifting onward in the soundless night, he was drawn into the lip of a sharply slanting trail. Here he halted.

It was the crossing, without doubt. A slim trail plunging into obscure depths. Keogh moved his body in the leather, watching the faint edges of the rock walls above him. So far so good. No ambush in the immediate neighborhood, for the claybank wasn't keening the smell of his own kind. But the bottom of the canyon was a different matter and Keogh cast up his chances with a cold precision. When he had done this and found the odds heavy on the wrong side, he threw the whole mess of reasoning out of his mind and moved downgrade with tightening nerves.

"Never get to the hills by lookin' at 'em," he grunted.

The trail shot to the edge of the abyss and swerved, running dizzily down a yard-wide fissure in the wall's face. To the other side was an unplumbed space into which the claybank's hoofs dropped crisp and sharp. Wind rolled through the canyon like a slow-moving stream and from somewhere emerged a thin splash of water. Keogh sat well back in the saddle, leaving the reins slack. The trail bit into the rock, reversed its descent and continued at an increased angle; and a few minutes later Keogh brought up with a swift checking gesture of his arm.

Warning. Nothing that he could see, for the blackness below was dense and solid. But out of the immediate area underneath came the faint smell of tobacco smoke. Shadders' men were waiting there.

"Tough," said Keogh, making a soundless whisper out of it. "Tough. But I'm glad to have 'em spotted after all this hide-an'-seek. Now—"

Naturally they knew he was coming. But, rapidly figuring the on-coming play as it ought to go, he thought they wouldn't open up until he was at the bottom of the canyon and well within the trap. Judging from the mealiness of the shadows down there, he roughly guessed the trail had another twenty feet to go before leveling off. How wide the canyon floor was and at what point the far trail started climbing, he didn't know.

"Claybank will have to take care of that," he reflected. "Well, didn't Tallen say it was tough gettin' through?"

Thus far he had maintained a critical, calculating calm. Now he let himself go. There was no more figuring to do. The black pit yawned at him; a cold fluid bathed his nerves and left him steady even while the whipping flame of an eager fighting temper consumed the last cautious thought in his head. Somewhere above the gloom the god of chance hovered uncertainly. Very gently, Keogh pressed the

26

horse and slid forward until he felt the trail edge off into flat ground. The claybank snorted, wheeled, threw up its head. Keogh bent far over in the saddle and jammed down his spurs. The claybank shot away.

He heard first Shadders' high yell. Then the voice became a small trickle of sound underneath a blast and belch of gun roar. Until that moment he wasn't sure where they stood but now he saw the jagged, spitting semicircle of muzzle flame on his left. They were all on his left and that first volley laced the ground just behind him—where he would have been if he hadn't put the claybank to a great burst of speed. Dust and powder stench filled his nostrils; lead broke sluggish and metallic against far boulders. Shadders had never ceased his half-screamed commands. As for himself, he clutched a cold gun in his fist. If they got the claybank it was time enough then to use it. Otherwise his replying fire would only bracket him.

They were working on the clatter of the claybank's hoofs, bringing up the aim. Slugs fell on the ground beneath him like dropping stones and one of them lashed at the saddle horn, going through the leather and hitting the steel core hard enough to rock him. The claybank faltered and came almost to a stand, fiddling one way and another.

"Damn you, horse," muttered Keogh, "find the way out of this. Go ahead, find it!"

The claybank veered. Keogh's leg scraped the canyon wall and high on his right arm a muscle began to burn. They'd pegged him. "Find it, claybank," he grunted.

The horse lurched forward, recoiled, slid around a high rock and got behind it. Keogh felt rather than saw the beginning of the up trail here and acting on the impulse he dug in his spurs again. He was right. The claybank went up, shoes flailing on the rocks. A gust of lead beat dully on the boulder behind him. Shadders' yell came across the dark clearly.

"Hold it—hold it! You'll kill Purvis!"

Keogh was well up the stiff trail when he heard that. The firing dropped to one or two stubborn explosions, then ceased. Turning a bend of the trail Keogh started the reverse half of the climb and got perhaps ten yards along when the claybank lost headway altogether, fiddling with uncertainty. Right ahead a solid and slightly moving shadow barred the trail.

This was Shadders' hole card; a man stationed here to block escape. And this explained the stoppage of fire below. The man's name, then, was Purvis and for some odd reason he held his fire.

"We'll both be killed," said Purvis slowly, "if they's any gunnin' done. Get off your horse and start back."

"You're some doubtful about takin' me?" parried Keogh, eyes glued to the shadow.

"Me? I ain't doubtful o' nothin'—"

The shadow of horse and rider swayed a little. There appeared to be a small space between the horse and the canyon wall. It was what Keogh looked for. Once more his spurs fell into the flanks of the jaded claybank and he lunged forward. Purvis tried to swing in and block Keogh, but the claybank's body made a wedge, a suddenly bucking, frantic wedge,

28

that pushed the other horse to the very edge of the trail. Purvis shouted, deathly fear in the cry and Keogh saw the man's torso sway; then the force of the claybank came fully against the other horse, and as Purvis fired, he and the horse tipped over the trail and fell. The claybank needed no more urging. It went up the remaining section of the trail in terrific lunges. Far below was a shout and an unleashing of gun blasts. Keogh topped the rim and galloped out to the black flatness of the desert.

He felt the claybank's trembling weariness but deliberately forced the beast on for a good three miles before drawing off and halting. Here he dismounted, sat on his hunkers and let his animal blow.

"That was the joker all right," he muttered. "I guess I've earned half of the hundred. Claybank, you'll do."

They were coming again and at top speed. Far to the north he heard the boil of hoofs. For a small interval he waited, then stepped into the saddle and sat motionless while the sound of Shadders' men swept toward him. On the point of shifting ground, the cavalcade seemed to change direction and presently swept past at a distance of three or four hundred yards. Later the rumble of their passage died out.

"Seems like nothin' is going to change that Shadders' mind," he reflected. "Right now he's bound for the settlement in yonder notch. He'll be there waitin' for me. My play—now what is my play?"

He debated this over a comforting cigarette. A man of wisdom would be making tracks for the far edges of this county, letter or no letter. But since he wasn't a man of wisdom and since entirely too much water had flowed under the bridge since dusk of this day, it appeared to be a shameful thing—quitting before he knew what he was embroiled in.

"I ought at least to have the satisfaction of knowin' why I'm bein' shot at," he decided. A sudden move of his arm woke a steady ache, reminding him of the bullet he had taken. Blood lay crusted a little below his shoulder point; his coat had a rent in it. The damage didn't, however, feel vital and he got to thinking of the dead Tallen.

"Poor devil figured he was hittin' back at Shadders when he sent me on this errand. I guess I better go through with it."

That was a sound excuse for continuing. So, putting the claybank to a leisurely canter, he laid his course by the notch now standing higher on the eastern horizon, and went ahead. Five miles on he was enveloped by the wings of a wide-mouthed valley. Another mile brought him to a turn with wooded slopes to either side. In the foreground one lone light made a yellow pathway through the opaqueness of the night. He passed a series of corrals, a sagging barn and came finally to something resembling a street. Here was the settlement, half a dozen buildings running irregularly along the bottom of the valley. While he watched, the light went out.

"No time now to hunt for Henry LaTouche," he decided. "I might go stumbling into worse grief. Better wait for day."

He turned from the street and rode along a

building's side, coming out into a dismal rear area. Dismounting here and unsaddling, he let the horse shift for itself on dropped reins and rolled up in the blanket, falling asleep almost underneath the clay-bank's feet.

He had set his mental alarm clock before sleeping and when he woke a kind of violet light came spreading down the valley. Saddling again and leading the claybank to the street, he went forward and settled on the edge of a porch. It wasn't much more than four-thirty, the settlement still locked in stillness. Lounging there as the violet half-dawn swelled to a rose-colored morning, he placed all the buildings carefully—stable, saloon, store, and a pair of dwelling houses. It didn't look like a dangerous place at this hour, but the ridges rising to either side of the town were thickly studded with pine, and these he studied with a long, thoughtful glance. Past the settlement the valley narrowed and bent into what seemed like high meadows beyond.

First to emerge from the houses was a lank and limp old fellow who straggled to the watering trough and washed in a sort of methodical care. Turning away from the trough he saw Keogh walking forward. Instantly the fellow stiffened, turned solemn and alert.

"I'm lookin' for Henry LaTouche," said Keogh.

"What for?"

"Letter for him," explained Keogh. "By the way, did a bunch of men ride in here last night?"

"Nobody rides here in the night," grunted the old fellow. "It ain't the habit. Where'd you come from?"

Keogh lifted his head to the ridges again, more and more observant. "Well, where's LaTouche?"

The man pursed his lips, put on his hat, shook his coat. "Go to the store and knock," he said, finally.

Keogh walked up the street and along the store's porch. At the door he made a tattoo with his knuckles and turned about waiting. In that short space of time the old man had gotten himself out of sight. Other people of the settlement were stirring. A second story window rose and a slim chap in a red undershirt looked down on Keogh. Somebody turned the saloon corner across the way, stopped and went back. The store door opened behind him.

He turned to face a man as tall as himself but in the middle fifties. Just out of bed, there was still a touch of blankness in the agate-blue eyes looking severely at Keogh. "Well," said he, "it's an early hour to be broachin' my store. What can I do for you?"

"LaTouche?"

"That's me."

"You know a man named Tallen?" asked Keogh.

LaTouche walked through the doorway, instantly alive. "You been in King's Plaza, sir? You saw Joe Tallen?"

"A friend of yours?" insisted Keogh.

"My partner," said Henry LaTouche. "I see. You got word for me."

"I reckon I have," agreed Keogh. "Last will and testament."

LaTouche bent forward, mouth and cheeks turning bleak. "They got him, sir?"

"Seems like they had him corralled down there. I gathered he couldn't get away. But he figured I might

32

make the grade. I busted clear. Last I saw, Tallen was blockin' off the town while I went out the back way. He went down scrappin'."

"Shadders—" said LaTouche with a cold bitterness beyond description.

"Yeah. Here's the letter Tallen asked me to give to you."

He reached to his inner pocket and brought the letter out, holding it toward LaTouche. For some queer reason LaTouche stood without movement, eyes fastened on the paper. Keogh heard talk behind him and the slamming of a window. The old fellow who had washed at the watering trough came leading a cow off the ridge. LaTouche stepped past Keogh and put an arm against a porch post. "Another sweep for Shadders. May his soul burn in hell! He got a man when he got Joe. Ain't much left for us now. I—"

The shot broke across the morning lull with a flat "spang," echo working back along the valley sides in long, dying waves. A woman screamed somewhere. Keogh, turning sharp on one heel, found Henry LaTouche sinking slowly to the porch boards. The man's face veered toward Keogh and he started to say something that never was finished. He dropped, as grim then as when he stood alive. A second shot's echo rushed up the valley and a bullet hit the porch wall behind Keogh, who swung, plunged into the adjoining window that he fell against, lifting his gun and poking out one of the glass panes. The settlement street was empty; a moment later a long line of riders raced down from the trees and came thundering through the street.

Keogh saw Shadders. He saw Sam Veen. He saw

33

twenty other dark faces. All guns were out as they took that street at top stride, smashing lead into wall, door and window. Keogh took deliberate aim at Shadders, but another rider came rapidly abreast of the big-bodied saloonman and Keogh's bullet rolled him from the saddle. Another rider fell almost at the same time, bringing to Keogh's attention the hard, furious answering fire from every angle of the settlement. These people apparently knew how to get into action without delay. Keogh tried another shot at Shadders but now the saloonman was well out of the street and blanked by his followers. A wailing voice said: "Wait—wait for me! Shadders—I'm hit!" But the tail of the raiding party faded down the valley, leaving behind four fallen men, a smoldering pall of dust and the reek of burnt powder. It was over as suddenly as that. Keogh reared up from his knees and mechanically threw out the cylinder of his gun. On the verge of thumbing in fresh cartridges, he heard a woman's voice break across the room as taut as a fiddle string.

"Drop the gun! Turn around—you!"

Chapter Three

When he wheeled—gun pointed at the floor—he found himself covered by a girl who held a cumbersome .44 steadily, almost carelessly, on the target of his chest. For a moment Keogh thought that she was very young, the smallness and litheness of her body accented by the whipcord breeches and the loose gray shirt open at the neck. But as the tight silence continued he corrected that impression. Beneath a head of ash-blonde hair were the features of a girl past the age of dreaming. Her face was clear, sharply defined and her eyes were a steady gray, at present full of an emotion that might have been either anger or grief, but which certainly wasn't fear. She was feminine and graceful to her fingertips, yet Keogh instantly felt that she looked upon the world as a man would.

"Drop the gun," she said.

He stood fast, holding her glance. "The mystery," he grunted, "grows deeper and deeper. Why should I throw down?"

Her head went back. "You come here. Shadders follows. I heard what you told Henry LaTouche and I don't believe a word of it. You're in with that crooked bunch. It worked too smooth to be otherwise."

"You saw me firin' at Shadders," Keogh pointed out.

"Sure—to carry out the story. Probably you shot at the sky."

"Don't believe in Santy Claus anymore, do you?"

She made an impatient gesture with her free arm. "I was born into this trouble. Raised on it. What do you expect me to do now—faint, scream, be ladylike?"

Something about her face had been reminding him all the while of another. Suddenly he thought he knew. "Look here—who are you?"

"Helen Tallen."

"Then this Joe Tallen was—"

"My father," said the girl, pressing the words through tight, colorless lips.

"Good Judas," muttered Keogh. Setting his gun in its holster, he reached for the letter he had jammed back into a pocket during the melee, and held it out to her. "I reckon you get this then."

She kept her position for a long while, searching him with a narrowed intentness, reading him through and through. And in the end she abandoned her guard over him with an odd shrug of finality, threw her revolver on a near counter, and accepted the letter. He saw her eyes race over the page, wink shut. A suppressed groan escaped her and she bit into her lower lip until a white shadow crept down it.

Whirling about she walked to a far corner of the store and though not another sound came out of her he knew she was crying in that deep, rigid manner worse than all the lament and fury in the world. The letter slipped from her fingers and dipped to the floor.

It left Keogh helpless, profoundly moved. A dull rage swept over him, a rage directed at Shadders and all that the man stood for. Going foward he bent to get the letter; having packed it all night and having seen the man to whom it was intended die at his feet, he considered himself rightfully entitled to know the contents. So he read the nervous sprawling handwriting on the single page:

Dear Henry: You and I have licked a lot of things in our time, old sport, but here's one play that's got us hipped and no mistake. We both been too stubborn to admit we was gradually being pushed to the edge of the cliff. It's so, Henry. I shouldn't have come here but it looked like our best bet. I figured Shadders might ease up, make a dicker for peace. The answer is I'm in King's Plaza and can't get out. I doubt if I ever will get out, Henry. Shadders is an Indian—he don't ever forget anything. My mistake, but I had to try it. Anything is better than what we been going through. Better face the facts, we're two old duffers without an army. The settlement is milked dry, all the good men dead or scared out of the hills. I'm writing this in the dark and can't even see the words I put down. I guess it's good-bye, friend. But if this gets to you it'll be brought by a man—a real man. Maybe he's the answer. Anyhow it's all the hope I can give you. Be good to Helen. Tough on her, but she's steeled to trouble and she'll weather through somehow. So long. We made a good scrap of it anyhow. Joe.

Keogh looked at Helen's rigid back. "Your daddy was a scrapper. I'll say that."

The settlement began to bubble with talk and Keogh turned to see men come up to the hotel porch. They walked in, solemn and rawboned men without much spring to their stride. Standing there, he waited until they made a semicircle around him—a dozen assorted figures, none of them very young. Obviously they were past the age of gambling and just as obviously they were shaken by a feeling of discouragement. With their entrance also came a feeling of defeat. It was the old man Keogh had met at the pump who took up the part of spokesman and inquisitor.

"It's kinder funny," said he. "Maybe you're right and maybe you're wrong, but this'll bear a lot of explainin'."

For answer Keogh passed over the letter. The old man read it, first to himself and then aloud. When he had finished he picked out one phrase and repeated it. "'The settlement is milked dry, and all the good men dead or scared out of the hills.' So that's what Joe Tallen thought." The old man looked about him. "Joe Tallen said that. He's got no more faith in us than that. Well, who was responsible for milkin' the settlement dry if not him and LaTouche? We backed those two men in every play they made, didn't

38

we? And what's left now but some empty buildings and a handful of people livin' under a cloud of death. Joe Tallen ought to be more kindly of his remarks."

"He'll make no more remarks," said Keogh. "Tallen was killed last night in King's Plaza."

The gathered citizens took this news in stony silence. Keogh saw them look toward the girl, now turned and facing them. Her crying was done, her cheeks smooth and expressionless.

"Tough on you, Helen," said the old one, and began moving around the store room uncertainly. It was obvious that Tallen's death hit these people hard, further sapped their courage. "But it leaves us in a jackpot," added the old man. "Shadders has put his two long standin' enemies out o' the way. He'll be feelin' strong now. He'll be feelin' like he can knock this settlement over at his free will and ride the hills like he pleases."

"Look here," put in Keogh. "What's at the bottom of this trouble?"

The old man's answer was to ask a question of his own. "You—does Shadders know you carried Tallen's note?"

"Certainly," said Keogh. "That's why he came here. He was on my trail all night."

"And he'll be on your trail from now till hell freezes over," said the old man. "If you stay here you'll draw down another attack."

Keogh's answer was sharp and definite. "Fine. We'll see to it he's well met next time. If he's fool enough to run against an armed camp, that's all to the good."

But the old man kept shaking his head. "We can't

stand it. No sir, we can't. It's gone on long enough. Both Tallen and LaTouche bein' dead, why should we keep up the battle? It wasn't our battle to start with. No reason why we should inherit the thing."

For the first time another of the group broke in—a younger fellow. "This man," said he, indicating Keogh, "has got to get out of here. Ride over the hill. There's the answer, Blinn."

Blinn—the old man—came to a stand. "That's the answer, all right. Young man, you'll have to get out of here."

Suddenly the girl broke in. "Wait a minute. You mean to drive him out so Shadders can hunt him down like a rabbit? Shame on you, Dad Blinn! Where's your pride? He helped my father—or tried to. And your answer is, shove him out on his own."

"Bein' a Tallen, you'd think like that," observed Dad Blinn gently. "What should we do?"

"Fight back," snapped Helen Tallen. "Never quit—never give up—never let Shadders' grip close down on this country!"

"We just can't go on fightin'," said Dad Blinn. "We're only a little handful. Better to make peace with him."

"If you do that," said the girl, "you'll regret it forever. He'll move in with his brutal crew and rule so cold-bloodedly you'll wish you were all dead."

"Maybe. But if we don't give in we're dead anyhow," pointed out Dad Blinn. "No, you got to pull stakes, young man."

"I was hopin'," drawled Keogh, "you'd make a fight of it."

"You got to go—now," said Dad Blinn.

Helen Tallen came forward. "If he goes—so do I."

Dad Blinn looked distinctly relieved, almost happy. Said he: "I won't deny you're another honeypot to draw Shadders here, Helen. Maybe it'd be just as well if you did go. Go back to your ranch."

Keogh looked at the rest of the townsmen in astonishment. All along that semicircle he saw a like relief. They were pleased, then, to have Helen Tallen out of the settlement. It dredged up a hot, indignant anger that fell flaming on their heads. "Why, you dummies! You weak, dispirited imitations of nothin' at all! Stand there and tell this girl to shift for herself! I've seen a lot of funny things, but this beats me. It certainly does." He turned to the girl. "Ma'm, if you are minded to let me trail along, I'd be happy about it. The sooner we leave these desperate characters to their tattin' the better for all concerned."

She looked at him with that same long, cool regard. "Get your horse and come by here. I'll be ready."

Keogh walked to the door and turned for a last shot as he reached it. "It'd be better if you gentlemen pulled out and left the settlement to me and Helen Tallen. I think we'd do a better job than the bunch of you put together. Ma'm, give us a couple boxes of rifle shells before you leave."

He went to the end of the street and got his claybank. When he rode back to the store the men were coming out and straggling away. Dad Blinn stood on the porch, saying nothing until Helen Tallen rode through a between-building space and wheeled beside Keogh. Then Blinn moved forward. "Good luck, both of you. Don't figure it's so easy to

41

cave in. It ain't. You're both young. I'm old and tired and I got to think of the people left here. And don't come back here, either of you. By tonight Shadders will have his feet planted in the hills—where he's wanted to be for twenty years.''

Keogh and the girl moved forward and at a steady canter left the settlement behind. A mile onward they passed around a bend and into a narrower part of the valley. The girl was plunged deep in her own thoughts and Keogh watched the trees to either side with a fixity that left no time for talk. An hour later the climbing valley leveled off into a park at the top of the hills—a summit meadow fresh with grass from which corridors led away to more rugged quarters of these Horn Peaks. The girl halted, turned squarely on Keogh.

"You helped my father and I'm thankful and grateful beyond words. But you have no real business mixing in my troubles.''

"You want me to pull out?"

"That's not the point," she said. "I shouldn't allow you into any more of our hill quarrels.''

"I bought a hand away back at King's Plaza," Keogh drawled. "It ain't played yet and neither you nor your dad had anything to do with that. Don't worry about me. I'm here because I want to be here.''

"Thank God for that!" breathed the girl. "I was afraid you came along just because you figured you had to. What is your name?''

"Bill Keogh. Now, this Blinn spoke of a ranch. Your ranch, I suppose. Got a crew there?''

"Half a dozen men.''

"Why weren't they in the settlement watchin' you?"

Helen Tallen let the silence drag. "My father told Nig Dant, who is our foreman, not to leave the ranch unprotected—ever."

"Ahuh. Well, better bust that way."

The girl indicated the direction with her arm and they set out again at the same deliberate canter. A slanting sun sparkled on a creek running through gravel; around this clear meadow the edges of the trees glowed a dark green. It was a fine land, fresh and valuable land. Keogh, still roving the points of possible ambush, asked another question.

"Ma'm, what's this all about?"

The girl looked at him. "You don't know?"

"Not a blamed thing."

"And still you're willing to stick it out? Bill Keogh, it's been a long time since I've seen a man ride along without fear or malice. The beginning—the whole thing started before I was born. Shadders wanted to marry my mother. He lost. He never has forgotten it. My father's had to fight Shadders ever since. I even think Shadders turned crook and outlaw boss just to even the score."

"But it ain't the whole story," suggested Keogh.

"No. The rest though is only added on to that beginning. Dad and Henry LaTouche built up this range. All the hills belonged to them. At the peak of their luck they had a hundred thousand cattle strung through this country. A big outfit. But Shadders played his game, biting in here, sniping there, stealing by day, killing by night. Working always on the edge of our range. Strengthening his own riders, putting spies amongst our crew. Twenty years like that, Keogh. Well, there've been bloody, open fights. And when war starts, business suffers. We won, but we never could quite crush Shadders. He'd run away and wait for the next chance. So it went, until good men wouldn't work on our place. It was the same as being tagged to die. Then my father went down to King's Plaza to see if he couldn't end it. You know the rest."

"But you've got a piece of the crew left," mused Keogh, already figuring out a plan of action.

"A piece of a crew," agreed the girl, without assurance. "A range fifty miles long, no beef, and a piece of a crew. The settlement used to be our town. It lived on our trade. Look at it now. The last Tallen ordered out."

"But you've got a few men left," repeated Keogh and fell into a deep study. Helen Tallen watched him with a grave glance.

"You'll break your heart if you try," said she.

He turned to her. "You're not wantin' me to try?"

Steel on steel. A flashing fury broke through the shadows lying deeply against her eyes. "Of course I want you to try! I'm not gentle or meek! I'm not civilized! My mother's been dead since I was five. I've been raised in the saddle, taught to swear and rope and take everything like it comes. You bet I want you to try! When I look back and think of all the good, fine men who died at the hands of this gunman, I know there's no death too easy for him. Shadders has been ghost, devil and every lasting threat in our family all through these years. His name and his brutality has cut a crease in my brain so deep it will never heal! Keogh, here I am, here's my ranch, everything I have! Take what you want and go ahead!"

"Then we'll try," said Keogh, drawling out his words.

They had put the meadow behind, filed through a wooded trail and now came out into a narrow park that ran due north into a higher, more tangled country. Keogh, never ceasing his sweeping scrutiny of the terrain, suddenly grunted and drew in. Away off to the left he saw a single rider circle a pinnacle and come forward at the lope. The man sat stiffly in the saddle and dust rose like small exploding bombs behind him. Keogh reached into his saddlebags, pulled out a pair of field glasses and adjusted them on the figure. Afterwards he turned them over to the girl. "Anybody you know?"

"Nig Dant," said she, allowing a moment's survey. "Our foreman."

Keogh took the glasses and replaced them in the saddlebags. His face, turned on the approaching foreman, shifted to a set and watchful impassiveness. Rather idly he asked the girl another question. "Your dad had a lot of faith in this man?"

"Lately," said Helen Tallen, "my dad had to take whoever he could get on faith. Nig Dant is a gunman. So are the rest of the men on the ranch. They have to be."

"Yeah," agreed Keogh. "It's always like that in a war. Cowhands go, gun slingers come."

Dant came straight on, pretty sure of himself. Keogh made a mental note of that. For a rider in a

45

hostile land, this foreman seemed certain of what he'd find. And as the distance narrowed Keogh began to distinguish the man's features. He was tall, spare. The rigidity of his carriage became even more pronounced. He held his rein arm high and his free arm hung loosely beside him. When he reached hailing distance he checked his canter and advanced more sedately. It was then that Keogh got his definite impressions. Nig Dant's face was deeply burned by the sun and considerably pointed—type of face Keogh had come to know rather well in his travels, being extremely thin-lipped and frozen into a reserve that bordered on unfriendliness. It was not a face built for swift changes of emotion, nor one that would break easily into a smile. The foreman's head was small, pea-shaped, and his ears lay flat against it. Wheeling in front of Keogh and observing the usual courtesy of putting his gun side away, he met Keogh's observation with eyes that were a startlingly blank pale blue.

"Dant," said Helen Tallen, "this is Bill Keogh."

Dant acknowledged the introduction with a short nod and looked at the girl. "Was worried when you didn't show at the ranch last night. Started for the settlement this mornin' and picked up sight of you just a spell back."

"My father," said the girl tonelessly, "is dead. So is Henry LaTouche. Shadders did it."

"Ma'm!" said Dant and threw up his head.

The surface shock was there, but Keogh listened for the deeper tone of astonishment and grief and couldn't catch it. Even recognizing the fact that paid gunmen couldn't be very moved by sudden death,

46

this Nig Dant obviously felt no deep regret. And very little surprise. Keogh wondered if Dant had picked up the news previously.

"You hadn't heard, Dant?" asked the girl.

"No," said Dant. "Good lord, ma'm, this is terrible. We better get to the ranch right off."

"Keogh is coming with us," added Helen Tallen. "He's helping me."

Dant's eyes slid across Keogh's face and settled on the horizon. "We need all the help we can get," he muttered. "Now, I think I better ride home one way and you people another. So's we can scout different parts of the hills. I'll be on the ranch when you get there." And, touching his hat briefly, he wheeled and put his horse to a steaming run. The trees on the right finally swallowed him.

The girl pointed to a different course through the trees and the both of them cantered forward. It was quite awhile later that the girl made a bitter observation. "Any one of our old hands would have cried at the news. Dant isn't that kind. You see Keogh, loyalty goes when we hire men for killing instead of cowpunching."

"Suggest we put on a little more speed and hit that ranch soon," said Keogh.

The girl's glance narrowed. "You're thinking that, already?"

"I've dabbled in trouble before," answered Keogh. "First rule is to sleep light and trust nobody."

They went single file through a belt of trees, wound down a canyon and labored up its northern side. Half an hour later this rugged country broke away to a low-lying oval of considerable extent.

Houses, barn, sheds and corrals stood in it; and behind them a cone-shaped peak reared its black crest a thousand feet nearer heaven. They cut down the containing slope of the clearing and crossed to the house; and when they turned a corner and halted at the house porch, Keogh saw eight men lounging there in plain attitudes of waiting.

Keogh's senses were sharp and swift-moving. One running glance satisfied him. He didn't like this crew. These fellows were all built in substantially the same pattern as Nig Dant, who stood a little to one side and looked silently on. They were dark and fiddle-footed. Utter stillness held them but behind that was the hint of nervous muscles. And not a single one spoke to the girl. Here was a challenge that even Helen Tallen recognized. Slipping from her horse, she walked up the steps and paused there.

"You men," said she, "had better know this now. Meet Bill Keogh. From this time forward he'll be in charge. Make no mistake about that. What he says goes—even with me."

Keogh watched her disappear inside the house and close the door. Stepping to the ground, he observed the yard with a slow thoughtfulness, feeling the hostility increase all around him. The men were saying nothing at all, but he noticed their attention shift to Nig Dant as if expecting him to meet the issue.

"So you're foreman and I ain't?" muttered Dant. "Quick change."

"Quick times," said Keogh, casually. "You found the ranch all right when you got back, I suppose?"

Dant only nodded.

"Let's get this clear," pursued Keogh. "Am I acceptable as a prod, or ain't I? Want to know just how I stand without delay."

"I guess you'll do," grunted Dant.

It was Keogh's turn to nod. In his head was still a wonder as to why Dant had felt it necessary to reach the ranch ahead of them. He thought he knew the answer, and as he strolled toward the corral nearest the barn his eyes roamed the earth. Quite a pattern of tracks led from the corral toward a high trail rising from the clearing and circling the nearby peak. Fresh dust smell clung to the air as if a group of men had recently ridden in or out. Going past the corral, he forebore looking behind him, but he felt the rest of the crew straggling after. Aside from the barn sat a long bunkhouse; as if moved by impulse Keogh went in. Smoke still circled against the ceiling and half a dozen glasses stood around an empty bottle on the bunkhouse table. This Dant, he realized, didn't enforce much discipline. On a well-organized outfit such a sight would have been impossible. The place was in a messy shape.

Reaching over, he took up a pack of cards and began riffling them in his fingers. The members of the crew came in softly; the door slammed. Turning about, he found himself barred from leaving by these eight hands. One glance convinced him of their attitude. Dant threw a cigarette to the floor and stepped nearer.

"We'll do a little talking, Mister Keogh. Maybe you're in the wrong place."

49

Chapter Four

"I figured this to come," drawled Keogh. "But not so soon."

"As how?" challenged Dant.

"What seems to be your big doubt?" parried Keogh.

"We don't know you," grunted Dant. "Who can tell that you ain't on Shadders' side?"

"The girl seems to figure my credentials ample," Keogh pointed out.

Dant waved that aside. "She's a woman. She wouldn't know."

Keogh made a clean shuffle of the cards, cut them, raised his head again. "Do I understand you to mean you'll override her judgment, Dant?"

Dant stood quite still, the pale eyes fixed unwinkingly on Keogh. Not by the least shift of a face muscle did he express an inward emotion. And he evaded Keogh's question. "It's odd," said he. "You're a total stranger. You rode into King's Plaza night before last. Immediate you get into a jam. You come to the

50

settlement. You work yourself into this job. It'll bear some explainin'."

"How do you come to know so much about what happened at King's Plaza?" Keogh wanted to know. "You were supposed to be up here in the hills."

Dant's lip corners sagged a trifle. Here and there, amongst the crew, Keogh saw a change of expression. "Never mind," said Dant. "I've got a way of knowin' these things."

"Then if you know what happened in that joint, you'll know why I'm here," Keogh pointed out.

"Not sure,"muttered Dant.

Keogh's eyes narrowed. "I don't get this."

Dant let the silence fall. It seemed characteristic of him to draw back into himself and wait, all the while searching Keogh with his centering stare, feeling his way through the situation, waiting for a slip. But Keogh matched the silence and Dant finally stirred and said, dryly: "I'll clarify things for you, Keogh. If there's trouble about here, we can take care of it. All us boys know each other pretty well. It doesn't set so good to have a plain drifter come in and try to take the reins."

"Go on, you ain't through," prompted Keogh.

The phrase flicked Dant's hidden temper. The foreman's frozen face cracked and a brittleness came out with his talk. "Better for you to ride away."

"Like I said," observed Keogh, "you're willin' to override the girl's judgment?"

"You want to make an issue out of that?" challenged Dant. "We can pull stakes and leave you alone. Then where'd you be?"

"Same place I am now," drawled Keogh, and

51

leaned forward. "That's a bluff, Dant. You wouldn't leave."

"Why not?" snapped Dant.

It was Keogh's turn to avoid answering a question. Instead he shifted ground. "Notice you had company before I came."

"Mighty sharp-nosed, ain't you?"

"Well, I been in hot water for twenty-six years. I ought to know some of the tricks, shouldn't I? You didn't have me pegged for a greenhorn at any time, did you?"

"What makes you think I didn't?"

Keogh met that curtly. "Because you're spendin' a lot of time on me here and now. You'd brush a greenhorn aside without comment."

"There wasn't any visitors," said Dant sourly. "The boys had been off on a scout and just got back." And after the echo of that explanation had gone from the room, Dant added a more insistent, more down-pressing phrase. "Don't you think you'd better bust the breeze, Mister Keogh?"

Keogh idly shuffled the cards again and laid them on the table behind him without looking away from Dant. The tension had gradually heightened. It showed plainly on the men of the crew. Though none of them had made so much as an open move during all this palaver, Keogh observed the stiffness of their bodies and the morose, brooding watchfulness of their faces. Cool and thoughtful, he considered this outfit. They had him blocked, there was no back door and not much room to shift on one side or another. Yet that was as much of an advantage as it was a disadvantage, for if a play came up he was cleared for action and they were badly crowded. Any bullet of his would reach one of them. Dant's lips had come together in a long, bloodless line and Keogh knew for a certainty the foreman was traveling along a similar line of reasoning. It became a matter of nerves then.

"I think I'll stick around," he said, softly.

Dant looked aside at the rest of the crew, snapped his head swiftly back to Keogh. He had made up his mind. "All right. Stay. But don't ask any help from us—and don't give any orders. I'll run things like I been."

He nodded at the crew and one man after another moved slowly out of the bunkhouse. Still standing by the table, Keogh watched the foreman's peaked shoulders recede.

Half across the yard Dant swung and walked into the barn, disappearing.

"So far, so good," muttered Keogh, and closed the door. "But not too good." He was badly placed. Dant flanked him from the barn. A pair of men paused at a back corner of the main house, which covered his other side. The rest were scattered and slowly shifting toward the front of the yard. Watching all this with shrewd comprehension, Keogh abruptly squared himself and left the bunkhouse. He was instantly warned that any act of his might crystallize the forming impulse of these people to have it out. Not a word was spoken, yet the two at the house corner straightened and all the men in the foreground turned, placing him into a ring of studying, sharp attention. Looking to his right and into the barn, he couldn't find Dant. The foreman had gone somewhere else—and this fact alone reassured Keogh and determined his procedure. It would need Dant's signal to start gunplay.

So Keogh plowed ahead, passed the two on his left, walked around the front of the house and climbed the porch. Before entering the house, he shot a sudden backward glance. The ring was dissolving; the play had missed fire. When he came into the room, Helen Tallen turned from a window and spoke swiftly.

"I saw all that, Keogh. You're right about Dant."

A rifle stood by the window, within reach of her. "Look here," said Keogh, genuinely alarmed, "don't you resort to any shootin', no matter what goes on. It won't help you at all. If you do, and I should take a bullet, they'd be mighty rough on you. Forget that."

She came forward and stopped directly in front of him. "Look here, Keogh. I'd have killed the man that killed you. You might as well know it now. If you are fighting for me, I'm fighting for you. Let's not argue about it."

He shook his head, watching the clear light of her gray eyes shine stubbornly at him. "You shouldn't," was his reply. "Leave the gun business to men like me, that have been singin' lead tunes most of their lives. We're burst with powder—damned with it. Keep clear of that. Never let the gun make you sorry the rest of your days. Leave it to me."

"I'd be sorry all my life," said Helen, "if I stood by and saw you shot down." Then she asked another question. "Have you ever fired without needing to, Keogh?"

"No—but plenty of times when I had to."

"What are we up against?"

54

"Looks like a state of siege to me. This Dant ain't quite come to the point of tryin' for me. But if I'm any judge of human nature, he will."

"Then he's in with Shadders. And where do you suppose Shadders is now?"

"Not far off," said Keogh grimly. "Now, I wonder. Is there any outfit around here that might come to your help if they knew you was in trouble?"

"None."

"No man that might take a chance and ride in to lend a hand?"

She thought about that for a moment. "No, I don't think so. We're at the end of the rope. After twenty years Shadders has shot them all away. All our help."

Keogh crossed to a wall and leaned against it, facing the door and puzzling out Shadders' tactics. Somebody had been on the ranch during the early morning and had gone. Warned by Dant. Why? It would have been simple enough to have laid a trap into which he and the girl would have ridden. That would have put an end to the affair—instead of prolonging it as now. There was an angle here he couldn't explain. The only certain fact was that Dant had orders to squeeze him off the ranch or lay him out.

The girl went down a hall, leaving Keogh alone. Going to the door, he looked out on an empty yard. An overhead sun poured steady heat into the clearing and the rearing peak stood bare and black to the sky. His watch indicated one o'clock, later than he had realized. Then, high up along the rocks at the base of the peak he saw a figure move, wave its arms, and drop from sight.

55

"You bet Shadders isn't far off," he muttered. "Time to fort up—"

Out of the back end of the house he heard Helen Tallen say swiftly, "Stop that! Let go—" And he wheeled and plunged into the hallway. A doorway led to the kitchen. Stepping through, he saw one of the crew—a saddle-faced man with sullen eyes—holding the girl at the waist and wrenching a stew pot from her hand. Keogh shot forward, struck the fellow a sledging blow on the temple, lifted him with a towering rage and smashed him into a corner of the room. The crash of that impact shook the house. A yell sailed over the yard and somebody came forward at the run; Keogh, alive to the nearing attack, motioned the girl aside and turned to face a rear door. Somebody kicked the door open. Nig Dant, chest rising and falling from his run, came through deliberately. Seeing his hand lying on the floor, he swung himself at Keogh, pale eyes wide and staring.

"The man took in more territory than he could cover, Dant," snapped Keogh. "You propose to back him up?"

"Never mind," said Dant. "You've got to get out. See? I'll not make another warnin'!"

"You know the answer," grunted Keogh. "How long does it take you to wind up, Dant?"

"Ma'm," said Dant, "he goes or we go."

"Go ahead," said the girl.

The hoofs of a single horse went beating away from the yard. Keogh resisted the impulse to go see which way the rider was heading, for Dant's pupils were so rigidly fixed on him that they seemed set in stone. The man was pulling himself together, making up

56

his mind again.

"One of the boys goin' up to see that fellow by the peak?" drawled Keogh.

Dant made no answer. Keogh's slim body creaked forward slightly and he spoke with a slurred gentleness. "Go ahead, Dant. You're twistin' your tail. Go ahead."

Dant's lips had a white shadow around them and his nostrils flared with the deepening fury that even the mask of his face couldn't hold in. But once again he drove his will to the breaking point and recoiled. He threw back his head, took a long backward pace and went out of the door. Keogh waited a moment before kicking the door shut and turning the key. "Never mind fixing anything to eat," he said, hurried and blunt. "If there's any more doors in the back side of this place, go lock 'em. Snap the windows. Go upstairs and lock everything that can be locked. Then come to the front of the house."

In the big room again, he stationed himself by the front entrance. The man who had ridden so quickly out of the ranch yard was now well up the trail that reached around the peak. Keogh saw the fellow's quirt come flashing down time after time and saw the staggering spurts of the pressed pony. Higher, the signaling figure stood on a boulder and waited. They were getting bolder, discarding even the pretense of caution. And one of the crew had led his claybank away.

The passing minutes were jamming up with trouble, Nig Dant's clear desire to shoot it out, the claybank's disappearance, and the meeting of those two on the peak's rocky base up there. Rolling a cigarette and drawing on it, a current of hot afternoon air running against his cheeks, he placed each fact of the situation where it belonged, casting out relentlessly those weak shreds of hope which were worthless to consider and fatal to lean upon. It was a one-man battle. It was Shadders and Veen and Nig Dant, with all their henchmen, against him. No favors asked, none given. Whatever Shadders' reason for standing off so cagily, it was gone now. The signaling from the peak made him sure of it.

He had the protection of the house, which was too large to hold. He had the girl on his hands. As a matter of straight defense he might reasonably expect to last as long as his bullets held out. No longer. But there was always the confession of weakness in letting the other man do the attacking; and if in the end the answer was sure defeat for him, then any counter move that he might make was all to the good. The player with the tall stack of chips could bet his hand conservatively, but the man down to his last few beans had to push his luck on the gamble for double or nothing. No use sitting in quietly and letting the ants eat him up. This was the rule of poker—a grand game that drew all of its wisdom and shrewdness from life, took out of men all that they had in them, and paid them back according to their merits.

When Helen Tallen came down the stairs she found Keogh standing slightly to one side of the door, brown face absorbed, eyes narrowed against the hot sun and the weather wrinkles deeply etched around his eyes. The cigarette was burned down nearly to his lips.

"What next?" she asked. "There're three or four

guns around here. Want them?"

He straightened and dropped the cigarette, crushing it with his heel. "Do this," he said. "When I go out of here, close and lock this door."

"Keogh!"

He checked her gently. "Whoa. I'll have to be boss of this."

"But, Keogh, I saw them from an upper window. They're waiting for you to expose yourself. Dant's standing in the barn with a rifle. The rest of them are hidden. They'll trap you."

"If a dog won't dig," said Keogh, "he'll never uncover any bones. You close the door and go back and guard that mug who's sleeping in the kitchen."

She started to protest again and stopped it with a sudden shake of her head. Keogh muttered. "You're a swell fighter, Helen," and walked out to the porch. The door closed softly, the bolt clicked.

He stood poised a moment. Nothing in front bothered him. All the ranch buildings were to the rear of the house and all Dant's men were there. But to his right, directly off the porch end about twenty-five yards, the close-warped bars of a corral afforded pretty fair shelter, and from that vantage point he could command sight of the barn, the bunkhouse and a scattering of sheds. It was the only place he could run for after leaving the porch.

"If it's going to be done," he muttered, "it'd better be done in a hurry. Shadders will come swarmin' down here pretty soon."

Putting himself against the house wall he walked almost to the end of the porch. One more step and he would be exposed. Exposed first to a tool shed about seventy-five yards behind the corral. Without doubt a man was stationed there and this man would see him first, followed by those in the bunkhouse; then Dant in the barn would pick him up and, lastly, those who were hidden in the store house back of the main ranch house. He figured none of these angles to be dangerous to him as he raced toward the corral, for the distance was a little too great for strict revolver accuracy; none of them excepting the barn, where, according to the girl, Dant waited with a rifle.

"He's the man that would think of a rifle," mused Keogh. Unconsciously, he rubbed his palms along the side of his legs. He lifted his revolver, opened the cylinder and thumbed a sixth shell; snapping it shut, he drew himself together and took one long pace forward, dropping off the porch. Immediately he broke into a run.

He had his eyes fixed on the shed behind the corral and it was from that point the first shot came. The door of the shed swung open, a ranch hand appeared, ducked to both knees, sun shining on a hatless, bald head. This one was taking a sighted aim with his short piece; Keogh had figured to save his lead on the run, but in face of the careful aim, he raised his own gun and whipped a slug at the man. The other's shot went wild, echo rolling across the clearing and rocketing up the high sides.

A flat, sharp report drove across the yard and he nearly stumbled as a jet of dust sprang up at his feet. That was Dant's rifle, with Dant calculating a little too much on Keogh's speed. Keogh was halfway to shelter and waiting for the second rifle shot with a cold constriction of nerves; but if Dant fired im mediately the sound of it was dimmed by the full-throated roar of all the other guns opening on him. He felt the lick of a bullet's wake, felt the impact of a bullet at his heels; and on that narrowing space between himself and the corral the dust rose like snake heads. He was within ten feet of shelter when Dant's rifle cracked again—and again missed. The long suspense in him broke as water might wash a dam away, and he flung himself behind the corral with an energy and a rage that boiled through his blood.

The firing slackened, but an occasional pellet flattened dismally against the bars above him. Dant yelled something he couldn't make out, but the next moment he rose and ran along the circling sides of the corral until he stood facing the side wall of the tool shed, masked from lead plunging out of the rear yard. Guessing that the man in there was crouched pretty close to the door, Keogh sent a shot through that part of the wall. A man came out, swerved and flung himself at Keogh, and when he lifted his piece to fire a strangling yell swelled weirdly from his throat. Keogh, weaving aside, shot him through the shoulder and sent him spinning to the ground.

The shed was his if he wanted it, but he avoided it for the trap it might become. Moreover, he had left the main house with the idea of attacking Dant openly and he didn't mean to hole up and let Dant seal him in like a gopher. Going forward, he took up the man's gun and threw out the chamber, replacing the empties with fresh loads. He did the same with his own revolver, meanwhile hearing the shed rumble like a drum as a strenghtening fire beat into

61

the far side. A rifle's tapered bullet ticked the corner of the shed, glanced off and went screaming on. Dant yelled again, this time clear enough to let Keogh catch something about circling the house.

That put him on guard, for if they circled the house and crept along the porch they'd catch him between fire. It was the old nut-cracker business. Sliding to the back of the shed he settled one of the revolvers against the edge of a board and lined it carefully on the porch. A moment afterwards he squeezed the trigger. A half-exposed body sank away.

All this while the possibility of Shadders coming out of the timber kept worrying him. Such a shift would mean a sudden end, and though the trail up there was still empty he was nevertheless prodded on by the threat of such a disaster. Nobody else was to be seen on the porch. Crawling along the rear of the shed, he put his head beyond the corner for a brief view and drew it sharply back. Diagonally across the yard he discovered three men standing side by side inside the wide door of the woodhouse more or less attached to the main dwelling. Those three plus the two he had hit made five. Dant was probably still stationed in the barn, the entrance of which was hidden from him by another intervening structure. That was six, and the man Helen Tallen had in the kitchen made seven. One man to be accounted for.

Studying it out briefly, Keogh figured the missing man to be either in that flimsy affair ahead of him—it wasn't much more than a lean-to—or else in the bunkhouse beyond. In any event he had to go forward and make his breaks, not wait for them. So, lifting his guns, he ran from the shed's shelter and aimed for the lean-to. Immediately he was bracketed by the three hands over in the woodhouse. They opened swiftly enough but the distance pulled their shots wide and his own covering fire was enough to disturb them. He flung himself back of the lean-to, peered between brittle dry boards and found the thing empty.

He had so far made a successful march of a good three hundred feet from the front of the yard on back toward barn and bunkhouse. These two buildings lay beyond the lean-to and as he went creeping forward with his body pressed well against the boards he felt his nerves go tight on him. Once at the edge of the lean-to and he would sweep all the coverts of the remaining five men, and in turn be definitely spotted by them. From that point on it would be a shoot-out.

But he never reached the corner of the lean-to. Within a hand's length of it, he drew up and grew still. Nig Dant walked slowly into sight, out from the direction of the bunkhouse. He was a good hundred and fifty feet away when he wheeled, faced Keogh and came forward with a slow, stiff step. And as he came he brought his rifle to his shoulder and took aim.

Keogh's brain seized one stark fact and crushed the truth out of it. At that distance he couldn't compete with Dant's rifle; but if he broke and ran forward he immediately put himself into the flanking fire of the other men over by the woodhouse. Retreat was just as bad, for they'd rush him and Dant's rifle would knock him over. The old nut-cracker game had worked for Dant after all.

In such a situation and with the odds so dead against him, Keogh reverted to his plain fighting instincts. Pitching up both revolvers he advanced on Dant, firing as he went. Dant's rifle kicked back, black smoke wreathing from the muzzle. But Keogh felt nothing and a furious, savage pleasure tore through him. Never daring a side glance, he heard the three at the woodhouse come out on the yell. They were firing, now, in front of him as if deliberately intending to ruin his nerve while Dant put in the killing blow. But as swiftly as this volleying began, it was blanked out by the over-whelming boom of a shotgun. A man cried like a child in agony and from another came a torrent of profanity. Keogh saw Dant falter in his advance and twitch his head toward the house. As for himself, Keogh lurched forward, putting his shots at Dant's feet. Dant stopped entirely and laid his cheek along the rifle stock for a final aim, the black snout of the gun staring at Keogh like a sightless eye. He broke into a run, while time seemed to stop altogether and the lesser sounds of the yard died from his senses. He listened for the crack of the rifle. Grim and reckless and uncaring, he listened for it. The sound never came. Keogh's raking shots lifted a screen of yellow dust around Dant's legs and one of them, speeding out of a belching muzzle, reached its target.

Dant shivered. The rifle veered and its exploded bullet went banging off in the general direction of the house. Then the gun fell and Dant, locked in a paralytic rigidness, looked at Keogh with dawning horror. Out of his throat came a rasping, baying noise. The foreman's hips crawled upward from the brush, and his peaked shoulders began to turn; and then he broke at the knees and plunged to the swirling dust, face down. He was dead when he struck.

Keogh swung around to guard against the rest of the crew. But he had no need to. Two of them were racing toward the peak on horseback; the third staggered after them from the clearing with his hands pressed against his head. The back door of the house opened and Helen Tallen came out, shotgun cradled in her arm.

"They started to rush you," said she, calmly, "and I stopped them."

Chapter Five

"I rise to remark you did," grunted Keogh, scanning the yard intently. "Get inside, Helen. There's one more man around here somewhere."

"No," said the girl. "That was Tabe Jukes. Never was much account. He ran away when you started from the corral. I saw him duck around the house. He's miles off now."

"How about the dude in the kitchen."

"Still out."

"Go watch him till I come back," said Keogh and walked back to the tool shed. The fellow he had pistoled through the shoulder sat with his head against the shed side. Seeing Keogh, he turned his face away, sullen and speechless.

"You don't know when you're well off," commented Keogh. "Get up and walk toward the porch—in front of me."

The fellow moved, cheeks twisting with the effort. Keogh stripped off his gun belt and pushed him on.

When they reached the porch, Keogh took one long look at the puncher huddled there and shook his head. "You might have been him," he added gently.

It was around two, with still no indication of Shadders in the higher trees. Rolling a cigarette, Keogh loitered a minute or so in the shade. He felt tired, now that the strain was over; tired and a little pessimistic. After all this thunder and fury he was still in the same position—waiting for Shadders to attack. It took considerable effort to throw the thought out of his head and to pull up his spirits again. There was a lot to do.

"Amble to the bunkhouse," he muttered.

The fellow went willingly and in fact seemed glad when Keogh told him to lay on one of the bunks. Catching a coiled lariat from a wall peg, Keogh cut it in half and tied Dant's man, first at the arms and then a full loop around the body and bunk frame. Afterwards he rummaged the place for guns, finding none. When he returned to the house, he found Helen covering the awakened prisoner.

"This man," said the girl calmly, "is Chuck Wing, and he's been sayin' things."

"Bunkhouse for you," ordered Keogh.

"We'll see what Dant's got to say to that," growled Wing. "Where is he?"

"The world turned over in the last half hour," said Keogh quietly. "While you was sleepin'. Dant's dead, my boy. Get to the bunkhouse."

He laced Wing to a bunk frame across from the other prisoner, though doing a tighter job, and left them together. "Sort of like a Rip Van Winkle case,"

67

mused Keogh. "He went to sleep in one situation, woke up in another. Lucky. There'll be more sleepin' before this thing is done—and less wakin'."

The full effect of the struggle was just now working through his system, leaving him restless, fiddling around, constantly roving the far trees with a narrow, glinting gaze. The missing Tabe Jukes bothered him some. There was just a chance the man might have returned to the ranch and hidden himself for a good shot. Using this as an excuse to be moving, Keogh began a thorough search of the premises. But all he found was his claybank and five other horses saddled to ride—placed here by Dant's men before the scrap began. He took the claybank and a likely looking black and led them to the kitchen door. Inside he saw that the girl had laid out a meal.

"Sit down," she prompted. "If we're ever going to eat we'd better do it now."

Keogh studied her. "Did anybody ever tell you, Helen, that you were a pretty good hand in trouble?"

"I said I was raised like a boy, Keogh."

"I don't observe it hurt you any," said he. "But I don't like you usin' a gun—"

"We argued that out once," she cut in. "Once is enough. I told you I'd fight for those who fought for me. Why don't you eat?"

He took up a sandwich realizing he had to do better; the weariness and irritability might show through and upset her. She was sharp-witted.

"Keogh, what's going to happen now?"

"Shadders will be along any time," said Keogh, knowing there was no use lying about it. He would have softened his answer to a girl of lesser courage. Helen Tallen didn't need coddling. She accepted his statement with a noncommittal shake of her head. "I sort of figured that, too. And we'll stick here and let them come?"

"Ever hear of Miles Keogh, Helen?"

The girl's attention focused at the mention of that name. "Sheriff Miles Keogh—Baron of Bayou County? My father rode with him as a young man. He used to tell me tales of Miles Keogh."

"My dad," said Keogh.

The girl's eyes widened with an astonished knowledge. "You're *that* Keogh—the one who wiped up Bayou after your father was killed?"

"Burnt with powder—damned by it," said Keogh slowly.

"Imagine!" whispered the girl. "Imagine such an impossible thing happening! The only man that could help me—and here you are! What brought you this far north?"

"Travelin' to get away from my reputation," drawled Keogh. "To get a little rest and quiet."

The girl made a swift motion of her fist toward the bunkhouse. "I understand now why Dant was so careful about drawing on you. He knew who you were—he was afraid. That's why he laid his trap."

"Stretchin' a reputation pretty far," mused Keogh.

"Your reputation is worth a posse, even this far up," said the girl. "And there's the answer to Shadders' being so slow to come here. He's afraid, too, Keogh. Of you. Of the chance you might have friends waiting somewhere. Shadders figures awfully

69

close, Keogh. He thinks way ahead. He may have believed dad had arranged a party to come in and smash him. There's your answer."

Keogh moved the dishes around the table absent-mindedly. "I only brought up my dad's name for a reason. The old man was a gray wolf and he tried to get some of the hardness and the keenness of his knowledge into me. I remember his favorite phrase. 'Don't hang onto a situation just because you're proud. Don't be afraid to run away if you can come back at a later time.' That helped me many a time. It applies now."

"Run from the ranch?" questioned the girl, one small wrinkle crossing her clear forehead. "Run and let them have it? Keogh, I don't like that."

"Remember," Keogh pointed out, "we can always come again. No point in lettin' them surround and starve us out."

"They'll burn the house," said Helen.

"Burnt house or burnt hide," said Keogh laconically.

She started to protest more vigorously but bit the words off, and after watching him a long moment she changed completely. "I said you were the boss. That goes."

"It depends on when Shadders comes. If it's before dark, we won't be able to run. But I know he's cagey. Probably he'll wait for night. Not far off now."

He was restless again, uneasy about the delay, the hovering silence. Even in this rambling place it was stifling hot, and when he returned to the front room and opened the door he could see the heat layers

70

shimmering from the earth. Mid-afternoon sun poured down, the towering peak cut a blackly barren silhouette against a brassy sky.

"Look here," broke in the girl, "you've been going hard ever since you left King's Plaza. And this fight was as much as a month's work. You're dog-tired and you show it. Go lay down on that couch. I'll sit on the corner of the porch where I can watch all ways."

Keogh grinned. "You think of everything, don't you?"

"I think of you," said Helen Tallen, and met his look with a straight, gray glance.

"The idea has merit," drawled Keogh, and strolled to the couch.

He had no thought of sleeping when he settled down, nor did he think sleep would catch him. He never knew when his muscles loosened and he fell off. The next thing he was aware of was a softly insistent pressure on his arm and the girl's voice.

"They're not coming yet—but it's dark, Keogh."

He reared up. The room was a dull black and he saw only her shadow bending over him. Going to the door he found the trees obscured by another moonless night. The peak and its surrounding terrain was only so much formless mass.

"Should have poked me in the ribs sooner."

"You were dead. I wanted you to get all the rest you could."

She kept still for a long five minutes. When she spoke again it was in an emotionless voice. "Where will we run, Keogh, and how far? If we never get back, then where to?"

It seemed odd, at variance to the usual matter-of-fact manner she had shown him thus far. She was talking now like a woman—uncertain and with a touch of fear. "Crossin' a few bridges we ain't reached yet, Helen?"

"Don't you ever do that?" she asked, almost defensively.

"Almost never," said Keogh, still and thoughtful. "My life has always been a sort of day by day affair. Never had time to think ahead. Things kept slamming into my face, as this business now. Why regret it, why worry? The bridges you worry about ain't often the ones you come to."

"I know. But this has been my only home, Keogh. When I leave it I pull up my roots. We're leaving by night, heading off into nowhere by night—"

"Lord bless you," said Keogh, gruffly, "you're about the best private I ever had in my army. If we can't make this thing stick we can keep goin' on over the rim. There's—"

Darkness fell out of the sky suddenly, like a giant cape dropped over them. And with its arrival Keogh felt a definite threat beyond the pall. Neither sight nor sound warned him, but still he felt it. So strongly, so urgently did it hit him that all at once he felt he had tarried too long. He wheeled, jumped off the end of the porch.

"No time to lose now. You lock the door behind you and go through the house. Get a warm coat and meet me at the horses."

He reached the horses before her, stepped into the claybank's saddle and held the other in readiness.

72

Something held her up while the moments passed and the evening deepened around the outlying buildings and made them obscure patches of black. Wind rose as unexpectedly as the night, a crisp wind out of the west. Waiting there, he thought he caught the dim rumor of sound born down the wind. The claybank's head rose and he wickered gently. There was trouble out yonder, things moving; the feel of it drummed harder on his senses. The girl ran from the kitchen, breath short and fast, and when she climbed to the saddle he heard the catch of emotion in her throat.

"Steady," he muttered.

"Never mind me—never mind! I was born here, all my happy days were here, and my sad ones. But I'm over it now, Keogh."

"Keep beside me and say nothing."

They went at a slow drifting walk, not out through the front yard, but sidewards. Thus they slipped by the tool shed, left it behind. Keogh changed direction again, retreating from the peak trail. The girl caught his purpose immediately and leaned near him whispering. "There's another trail we can use, right of the peak."

"Head for it."

His senses were alive to the last cell, sucking like sponges at the gloom around him. Clearer and clearer was the feel of men off beyond the curtain. They were crawling in, they were creeping forward as silently as he fled. The girl moved a little ahead of him, pointing more to the south, her shadow swaying from side to side. Gradually they were drawing clear of the house, but with each passing moment, Keogh's nerves tensed and the conviction that they were being surrounded increased. Suddenly and startingly the conviction was verified. Dead ahead of them a match light burst like a bomb, glowed in front of a hawk-like face and went out.

The girl's breath came out of her in a short gasp. She stopped instantly. But Keogh, knowing now that Shadders' men were advancing in a wide, semicircular line, moved straight on to that point where the light had been. The man's carelessness had given him his fighting chance and he took it with a ruthless, cold purpose. He urged the horse to a faster stepping, brought up his gun.

The man's shadow and the man's voice broke through the shadow together. "Who's that?"

Keogh wheeled slightly, coming abreast the man who had checked and grown still.

"You confounded fool," grunted Keogh. "Don't you know better'n to expose us like that? Keep your matches in your pocket and go on."

The man's breathing increased and he grumbled half a reply. Keogh never paused. He rode by, the girl beside him. But another rider came from somewhere at a trot and spoke to the careless one with a bitter, suppressed rumbling. "You—who lit that match?"

The careless one snapped an answer. "How many times am I goin' to be bawled out?"

The rumbling voice grew louder. "Who else is driftin' over there?"

It was Shadders, roused and suspicious. Keogh throttled the impulse to sweep into a dead run and

74

calculated his situation rapidly. Probably he and the girl had passed through the line of advancing Shadders men. Shadders himself was about a hundred feet away. The rising edge of the clearing was only a spurt off. He didn't know where the mouth of the trail came in but the girl might be able to hit it without extra searching. If she didn't—

"Stop right where you are!" bawled Shadders. "You—yonder!"

Keogh leaned toward the girl. "Break for the trail," he muttered and slashed her pony's rump with his flattened palm. The horse leaped away, claybank rousing to a quick burst of following speed. Shadders' words became a volcanic stream of wrath.

"They got through, damn your souls! Turn around! Come on—come on you damned pinheaded fools!"

A gun roared. Shadders cursed it to silence and from the volume of that raging voice Keogh knew the lawless saloonman was in full pursuit. The girl's horse threatened to leave the claybank behind and for a long interval Keogh lost sight of her. Then he pulled the claybank up with an iron fist. Girl and horse were turning in front of him.

"I've missed it!" she called back.

"Take it easy—try again."

He turned the claybank. The girl shot away again, and from the right-hand foreground he heard her cry out sharply, "Keogh—Keogh!" All the drumming of these pursuing hoofs rose above the strain and heave of his own horse as he guessed Helen Tallen's location in the swirling black and galloped on. He found her again, almost running her down. "Up here, Keogh!"

She was rising with the trail, a rocky trail glinting with sparks as the shoes of the black flailed down. Keogh followed. Fifty yards higher he ventured a glance behind. Shadders' men had found the trail, too, and were driving recklessly into it. He couldn't see them, but he caught the telltale flash of iron on rock. Then the leading man of that following line— Shadders without a doubt—began to open up. The purple-crimson muzzle light danced across the abysmal night curtain.

Chapter Six

The girl seemed to know this trail perfectly and ran along it without a break of pace. The claybank followed confidently, great chest swelling as he took the stiffening grade. But the pursuing riders were losing ground, crowded by their numbers and probably hindered by Shadders' uncertainty as to what lay ahead. It was a rough trail and full of potholes that shook Keogh violently as the claybank stumbled in and out of them; it was a bending, increasingly uptilted trail. Once it swept around a hairpin curve and Keogh heard Shadders' men directly below him, so that he might have dropped a rock on their heads. Then it bent again and passed between rock shoulders, against which the hoof falls rang clear and loud. The wind sharpened, coming by the peak like flowing water.

As the moments passed Keogh watched the higher outline of the peak and found that they were gradually swinging around it as they penetrated the more rugged hills. Presently they were in timber, and presently out of timber again. Only once in that first quarter hour did the girl speak, to warn Keogh of a changing direction. Keogh slackened speed, the claybank veered; the pitch of the trail fell downward. Another fifteen minutes went by before Keogh called for a halt.

The horses were blowing. From the higher distance came a muffled, far-off tapping of fast traveling ponies; and a single gunshot's echo undulated across ridge and canyon.

"They've lost us," said the girl.

"We're going north along the spine of the hills?" asked Keogh.

"Yes. North. But we're not following the summit line. We're below it. This trail works out of the hills. It will put us out of the Horn Peak country by morning."

"We're not leaving the Horn Peak country," said Keogh.

Helen Tallen didn't understand this and said so. "Aren't we running away?"

"Not that far away," replied Keogh. "Didn't I tell you we'd fight again?"

"Why did we run at all, then? How can we fight here, against all the force Shadders has?"

Keogh kept silent a little while, listening to the rumor of the pursuing band. Sounds came back to him from different points. Shadders had split his crew. "It's like this, Helen. The whole point of fightin' big odds is never to let the heavy side freeze you in one place. We shift and we duck. We keep these men on the gallop. We work for a break."

"He must have twenty riders," murmured the girl.

"Makes no difference—"

One of the fragments of Shadders' bunch was approaching on the left rear. Keogh spoke swiftly. "Go ahead. But take the next trail you find going up. Keep workin' to the top of the crest. Head for the broken country."

They went on at a slower pace, riding through some darkling glen. A spraying falls sent its mist over them. The girl warned Keogh again and the shadow of herself and her pony merged with utter blackness ahead. For a while Keogh's only guide was the clacking of hoofs in front of him. They were going up again and during the next ten minutes no echo of pursuit reached them. But at the end of that time a fresh reverberation beat out the night. Another party sweeping along from a different point of the hills. By now the girl knew what was expected of her and she promptly cut up the side of a gulley and threaded a dismal stand of pines. So the better part of an hour went by, this game of hide-and-seek continuing. Sitting alert, Keogh swept the night with straining ears. Shadders seemed to know this country perfectly, for as time went on the out-reaching reports grew more pronounced. Comparing them thoughtfully, Keogh recognized the brutal saloonman's tactics. Shadders was throwing an irregular ring around the peak, blocking off the trails.

A colder wind struck him. To his left the cone of the peak stood dim and lonesome to the sky. They had at last made a half circle and were on that side farthest from the ranch. They had also reached the crest of the hills, for the area was flat, deeply pocketed and slashed by the rock rubble at the base of the peak; and from the immediate foreground emerged the rush and grumble of a high-level stream. Helen Tallen went on cautiously through the broken footing until the shadowed slash of the river was visible over the pointed ears of the horses. There she reined in.

"What now?"

"No crossing?"

"River's too swift, Keogh."

"And the peak at our backs," he reflected. "There's two ways blocked off. The trail we came up on is probably guarded by now. So that leaves us only the north side open.

"Want me to go ahead that way?"

"Rest awhile. We've made our move. Next is to see what Shadders does."

"There's caves around here, Keogh. Good hiding. Listen—I hear them off there. Off to the north."

Keogh, listening, picked up the shift of animals in that direction. "The man's a real Mexican general," he grunted. "Knows this country like a book."

"He ought to," said the girl bitterly; "for twenty years he's used it to fight us."

"We'll play dead and see what he thinks of it," Keogh murmured.

They got down and settled on a rock. After a half hour the wind turned uncomfortably cold and the girl slid into a protecting crevice. Keogh squatted on his heels, doggedly patient, scouring the night for sounds. Somewhere a part of Shadders' outfit still scouted. A shout rode down from a higher part of the peak. Then a lull of man-made noise descended and the boiling of the water seemed to increase. It was long after when the girl spoke from her cover. "What time do you suppose it is, Keogh?"

"Small hours of the mornin'."

"That much? It seems only a little while since we left the ranch."

"Fast movin' seems faster."

"Keogh—how can you play yourself against all that Shadders has? Twenty men. Maybe more."

Keogh answered slowly. "Numbers don't count. A stalk of wheat has a lot of kernels. But cut the stem and the kernels dry up and fall off. Get Shadders and his gang will split. Always that way with the bad ones, Helen. They're dangerous as long as they've got a real tough man whippin' 'em forward. When the bad one dies the gang won't hold together. It's every fellow for himself then. I've seen it go that way a dozen times. Shadders is powerful because he is a natural leader. He can hold men together. Make 'em fight. Pay 'em with good loot. But he's the only one, the only real leader. If there was another leader in that bunch he wouldn't stand for Shadders doin' all the bossin'. There'd be an inside fight. The gang would split or one of the two tough ones would die."

A leaden half hour passed before she spoke again. "Keogh, when you said that you sounded a million years old."

"The gun is a hard master," muttered Keogh, "and killin' is the oldest trade. The lessons you learn from

81

huntin' men, or bein' hunted by men, cut deep scars."

"You're sorry to be in this mess?" she asked suddenly.

His answer was quick and full. "Not for a minute. I was born to do this. Long ago I discovered the gods had made a gun singer out of me. When I woke up to that fact I made one rule which I've never broken."

"What was that?"

"To be a good gun singer—and not draw till there was cause. So—"

He broke off, rising and walking beyond the horses. A small core of light sprang out of the night, four or five hundred yards to the north; a core of light that reached out as the moments passed and thrust raveling points to the sky. A watchfire. Keogh turned about, suspicion forming instantly. Another light appeared downgrade to the east, on the edge of the pines they had come through; and as if the first fire were a signal, still more points of flame sprang up. They created a sort of three-quarter circle, ending in a fresh blaze on the upper slope of the peak. On the fourth side lay the river, a better barrier to flight than any fire. Another single shot echo exploded near the first fire to the northward. Keogh swung and walked back to the girl, hearing her quick exclamation.

"They've got us sewed up, Keogh!"

"I worked for a break," said he briefly, "but I didn't get it. So—next thing is to work for another."

"But—"

"Stay there, Helen."

He crawled over the rocks until he stood at the

margin of the river. Lying flat on his belly he tried to gauge the velocity of that tumbling water. He dropped a rock and heard it strike solidly a moment afterwards. Moving parallel to the edge about ten feet, he tried another rock. His extended arm touched a ragged, slightly sloping wall. With that much knowledge he returned to the girl.

"You know where to find one of these caves you mentioned?"

"We're just a few feet from the mouth of one now. Why?"

"Go into it and stay until I come back."

"Where—"

"Remember," he reminded her gently, "I'm still boss."

She rose, touched his arm. "All right, Keogh. Give me a gun. When will you be back?"

"After daylight," he said, pulling the rifle out of the boot on the black horse. Handing it to her, he added a warning. "But don't expose yourself by firing. Get into shelter. I'll wait here till I hear you call."

She paused a moment, the pressure of her fingers tightening around his arm and then relaxing. He heard her groping across the rocks and five minutes later caught her muffled, "All right." After that he led both horses several yards off and left them, taking his own rifle from the claybank. He took his lariat, too, and with his pocket knife cut off a section of rope about as long as his arm-spread. Working in absolute sightlessness, he tied the strip of rope to both ends of his gun, making a sort of sling. Then he adjusted the

83

gun over his back, fixed the rope under one arm and over the other shoulder. That much done, he returned to the edge of the river and let himself down into its uncertain depths.

He had already figured this to be the only way. The watchfires were close together and he knew Shadders' men would be stationed between them, waiting for him to come through. How Shadders had so certainly located himself and the girl was a puzzle which could be explained only by the exact knowledge this saloonman had of all the peak country. In any event, running the fire line was out. It had to be done via the gorge of the river—if at all. The breaks of the game had gone against him; as a man working with short odds he knew he had to expect this, double his bet and try again. And this try, he realized, would be near to the last. He no longer had the mobility of his horse to depend on, the girl was inside the ring, and morning threatened to break over the eastern rim. Shadders, playing always a cold and careful hand, had brought about another cornering situation. Shadders was a good fighter, a relentless fighter, and with ample power to carry out his brutal will.

He hung from the rim with his hands, feet lightly lodged on a minute shelving. Bracing and catching a fresh hold, he descended again. The river spray played on his legs and for a little while he thought he had judged wrong. But his exploring boots finally touched solid stuff and he let go, standing on rock with the full roar of the stream in his ears. Pressing against the slippery side, he put out his feet one at a time; and so he went downstream, forward, testing each step. He inched himself around an out-thrust point, heels-plucked by the water; he went a little more rapidly on a strip of gravel that all of a sudden plunged up to his hips into a riotous pool.

When he got out of this, his black temper was fighting down a touch of that fear which every man possesses when close to dangerous water; and he went with a more roused caution along another and somewhat wider strip of shelving. A glow of light flickered on the wall across-stream and from this he judged he was gradually coming abreast the fire he had first observed. The bank at this point appeared to rise higher. Twenty more tedious paces onward and he reached a point without foot-hold, without hand-hold.

Not in all his patient exploring could he find passage. The racing current whipped around his feet and boomed against sheer, slippery sides. And as he listened he thought he heard a deeper and more cataclysmic thunder below, as if the river raced over a ledge, or as if the crowding current was warring through great obstructing boulders.

He had reached another dead end in the fight. But all thought of retreating was out of his head and the same devils of temper that screamed at him in every tight, black moment of his career, woke now. He slipped the holster flap over his gun and secured it, adjusted the rifle on his shoulders, and jumped.

The current gripped him, sucked him down, shot him onward. Still under and clawing out with the one idea of keeping himself near the bank, he felt a submerged object smash his side. He came up, took a strangling breath and was dizzied by a succession of rollers that hurled him forward like a chip on a flood. He sank again, was ripped by currents that crossed from right to left. The thunder pounded harder on his ears, he felt himself go head first, down and down to the depths; when he struggled blindly back he was shaken by a terrific wrenching counter current that checked his wild turning and his onward progress.

Suspended, literally held half out of the water by these two opposing thrusts of the river, he tried to orient himself. But it was only the briefest of tries, for all things happened now in vivid half-seconds. He was canted aside, shot out into a long, curling pathway; his feet touched bottom and one final shove of the mad river sent him staggering into slack water. He waded two or three steps, reached a gravel beach, and fell flat.

He never knew just how long he lay there, vomiting water out of him. But finally, empty of stomach and light-headed, he pulled himself to his feet and looked uncertainly about him. His side still ached, his ears rang. One thing he noticed immediately, however, and that was the gray, mealy light breaking across the sky. Day was coming. Afterwards he saw the reflection of the campfire farther up the river. He had been carried considerably past it.

His first thought was for his guns and when he found them still on him he walked along the gravel until he touched the steep wall. Searching it, he found a rough projection. After he had pulled himself to this projection his reaching hands hooked over the rim of the wall, and so he left the river behind him. The fire was about two hundred yards south of his position and the glow of it flickered across a tangled area, outlining the jagged boulder points and the sagging depressions. It was the same sort of terrain he stood on, the same sort of terrain his turning eyes saw all about; and back of him, as far off in that direction as the fire was on the other, a small broken-topped butte reared its head into a rapidly lightening sky. Keogh measured the distance from butte to campfire and made up his mind.

"Within gun reach," he muttered. "That's where we'll sit out the next deal."

It was a good ten-minute scramble to the foot of the butte and another ten minutes to the summit, made a little ticklish by his knowledge that these crevices were fully tenanted by rattlesnakes. When he arrived at the butte's upper surface the clear sunless light of early morning had come and he began to see figures shifting in the distance. But for the moment he was absorbed by his surroundings. The rear edge of this butte seemed to drop sharply, a fact explained when he crossed over and looked down a sheer cliff which ended in the black waters of the river.

"Better than I figured, and worse," he mused. "They can't come up behind me—and I can't run out. Now—"

Returning to the original position, he surveyed the falling slope. Directly in front of his position the rock field was fairly uniform in contour. Nobody could approach him that way. To the left-hand angle of the butte, however, a much more rugged arrangement of boulders made fine cover; and on his right, next to the river's edge, another such granite tangle afforded shelter to an approaching man right up to the rim of the butte. He had, then, two flanks to watch. But as he raised his eyes and looked over to where two lone horses stood—his claybank and the girl's black—he knew his shift had been necessary. That yonder area was hard to defend. Shadders must have known as much when he threw his men around it, figuring evidently to drive his quarry in one of the caves.

"I'll fight from my ground instead of his," said Keogh and, pulling his rifle down, he settled on the ground and leveled the weapon on a gray patch near the smoldering fire.

It was pretty close to five hundred yards and they were moving behind a natural barricade protecting them from the peak area. And they were turned from him, not yet suspecting he had slipped free; moreover, the general stir they made indicated some sort of business, some sort of attack. Thinking of Helen Tallen hidden beyond, Keogh took deliberate aim slightly to one side of the figures and squeezed the trigger. "First is warnin'," he told himself.

That bullet drew a whole line of posted figures upright from the crevices. He saw some of them break, some of them stand facing him. Grim and stolid, Keogh drew down on one of those still figures and let the hammer fall. The man threw up both arms and pitched over. The line of figures collapsed.

"Should have been Shadders," grunted Keogh, morosely. "There's one man's pay for followin' the wild bunch. More sleepin' and less wakin' this fine mornin'."

Then the distant line rose, came forward irregularly twenty paces or so and faded again. That time Keogh had counted. "Seventeen. Not so many—but enough." He saw an arm wave from behind one of the rocks and on this rock he sighted the rifle, taking up the trigger slack. The line rose, charged forward. Keogh's muzzle veered slightly and kicked up as the bullet went banging into the still, cool air. The targeted outlaw collapsed and began to fall. All the rest of the attackers went down, save one; and even at that distance Keogh recognized the big frame of Shadders who motioned forward and kept coming. In straggling twos and threes the rest broke out of shelter and ran on. Keogh jammed his bolt home and tried for Shadders, but the saloonman, shrewdly guessing his time right, fell before Keogh could fire.

"Good enough," muttered Keogh. "I'll save the bullet."

They were all out of sight once more, and the interval of concealment dragged out. Trying the trick of spotting his target, Keogh lined up another rock; but when the gunmen rose again, only about seven came forward. The rest stuck fast, including the one behind Keogh's target rock. This time he took snap aim at another, fired and missed. The seven dropped and immediately the echoes began to roll and rocket across the morning. A piece of flint flew up in front of Keogh. Puffs of powder smoke rose out of those pockets where the rear outlaws had stationed themselves. After that first volley a silence settled, then they began firing again and Keogh saw the forward seven come ahead, all converging toward a tall cairn in the foreground. They reached it and disappeared before he could line his sights.

Meanwhile the covering fire strengthened and more rock chips hopped around him. Rolling to a little better protection, Keogh studied the pillar closely. Shadders had made one division of his forces and probably he was about to make another. In any event, somebody'd have to come out from behind that pillar; and on the right edge of the pillar Keogh laid his arm. He had three shells left in the magazine and a handful in his pocket; after that it would be revolver distance.

A nearer hit caused him to pull his head back just as two men dived away from the pillar—one to the right and one to the left. Keogh let them come without argument, figuring to make them a little careless on the next run. When they went down, he understood the game. Shadders had surveyed the butte slope and had also seen that the middle portion was too smooth to tackle; his strategy now was to work into the rougher surfaces on the extreme right of his position. And as thoroughly as Keogh despised the gross saloonman for his brutality and blackness, he had a moment's feeling of admiration. Shadders was himself leading off to the right.

Keogh started to line up his sights on the rock Shadders had dropped behind, but on second thought shifted the muzzle back to the pillar again. Old Miles Keogh, his father, had fought Indians and from that hard warfare had had his lessons in mass attack. Keogh had recalled what the old man had once said: "When a lot of 'em is rushin' you, never mind the front bucks. Ketch those behind followin' up. Keep the main herd from supportin' the forward ones and you can deal with the forward ones at your leisure."

Shadders had thought of that too. Keogh saw the saloonman come out and forward again, but the center of his vision ran along the sights and he saw a fellow leaving the pillar, running in Shadders' footsteps. Keogh fired, saw the man drop. Shadders had taken to shelter again, and so had the forward attacker on the other flank. But alone and bold, a gunman rose from the rear firing line, stepped around an obstruction and came straight ahead at a walk. Keogh took aim, wondering and regretful. The fool was mad—stark mad. The volleying ceased and a high yell came across the distance. "Come back here, Lace!" The man below twitched his shoulders and pulled up his rifle. Keogh swore bitterly and sent his bullet crashing down. Lace collapsed.

"A little embroidery that'll turn yellow soon enough in hell."

He had let Shadders and the other advance man alone, but they had both reached the rough stone rubble on their respective sides and from now on he had them to face. Both would be climbing in full protection, both would converge on him at the rim of the butte and rip at him with angling fire. But as he lay silent and watchful, he saw that Shadders could actually arrive at the rim without exposing himself, while the other man had a last twenty feet of the climb to make in partial open. This fellow first.

He tucked his gun against his body and rolled over and over toward the left. He reached a sheltering parapet of the rim, rose and crawled on his knees. Down the jagged crisscrossed surfaces he saw first a hand lift and fall and then a face crooked upward; the strained, sweat-streaming face of Sam Veen. Sam Veen's lips worked over his wolf-fanged mouth and he sank into his shelter again. But he had seen Keogh flattened out, gun still half under his body from the maneuvering; and working on that killer's chance, Veen reared out of his crevice and began to fire. Firing before he had his revolver pulled up. Keogh let go the rifle and reached for his holstered piece. Two rolls of dust marked Veen's low shots. Veen's eyes burned lividly at him and a third bullet scraped Keogh so closely that he felt the whip of it as his own hampered arm snapped into position. He saw Veen's gun swerve for the final shot and when his own gun's roar came flooding back at him, barrel so close that the recoil sent the hammer point into his forehead, he saw Veen's eyes flood with an emotion he had never known before.

But he had no time for a thought about it. Even as he reared, got to his feet and paced into the depths of the butte top to mask himself from the long distance shells still raking the edge, Shadders flung himself onto the rim and started to charge. He had his head lowered, but when he found Keogh, placed and waiting, he threw himself back on his heels and roared his insolence across the fifty-foot strip.

Keogh's gun hung in his fist, idle and point down. Shadders' weapon was half raised and rigid in that attitude. Cold again, nerveless, and seeing nothing but the white checkers on Shadders' shirt, Keogh listened to the sound and let the significance of the words go by. All that had gone before was but a preliminary to this. Shadders was an animal. An animal in every cruel, treacherous sense; but to this primitiveness, the brain of a man gave an unfathomed power of evil. Watching those white checkers, Keogh thought this, calculating on the moment that slanting gun muzzle would rise and spew.

"Keogh!" yelled Shadders as if he meant to say something more. But it was a trick to draw Keogh's attention aside—a trick of that brain teeming with tricks. Keogh's own gun rose when he saw the other's flash up. Terrifically swift. A blur and a roar. Shadders had fired—and Shadders had missed, at fifty feet. Keogh's eyes were on the white checkers as he fired in return. One of these checkers began turning a deep red and Shadders' big body began to curve aside. The saloonman's face was dull, falling away to the blankness that means neither thought nor life; and then Shadders went backward, over the cliff and out of Keogh's vision.

From the distance rang a long, high yell and it woke Keogh from his stillness. Running back to the left quarter of the table top, he got to his knees, crawled as far as the rifle and leveled it again. The fight wasn't over, but he thought he knew best how to end it. The chief had gone down in view of all; nothing now but to strike a last blow that would complete the wreckage of a gang already shaken by a treat of its own violence. Beyond the line of rocks where these men lay entrenched stood their horses. Pitching up, Keogh began to place his shots amongst the beasts. He fired the last shells in the gun, opened the chamber and thumbed in another fill. He began again, seeing the horses pitch and break out of the huddle; and then he located figures running back; crawling in caution, stumbling in haste. They were afraid of losing the horses, of being caught here afoot. Keogh knew how they looked at it, because he knew the heart of an outlaw. It meant nothing to them that they were still strong, still facing only one man. It meant everything that they had been smashed badly, that Shadders was dead.

Keogh changed his aim from the horses and harried the heels of the fugitive men. He saw them come to their mounts, swing up and race away—race down trail to the east. When he rose and descended from the table top, they were gone, leaving behind riderless saddles; over in the shadow of the peak one rifle kept up a slow methodical fire.

It was Helen Tallen. Crossing the distance slowly— for the weariness of spent energy left him gaunt and hollow—he found her standing on a rock, gun thrown at her feet.

"It's empty," she said. Then she came off the rock, crying: "Keogh—Keogh!"

He held her while she checked the storm inside her. And he drawled on about nothing much until she lifted her head.

"Keogh—they're headed for our house."

"Not those outlaws," said Keogh. "Not today. Another day, maybe, but don't worry about today. They're long gone. Just fast movin' shadows behind the dust."

"Another day? Keogh, how long is this to go on?"

Keogh smiled a little. "I sorta said that to insure myself a steady berth on the ranch, Helen."

She looked at him, the steady gray glance holding something of deeper importance. "In the beginning, Keogh, I told you to take the ranch, to take me, to do what you wanted with any or all of it. That still goes."

"In Bayou County," said Keogh, casually, "I know ten young men who'd burn the breeze to be punchers on a ranch like yours. We'll go home. Then I'll ride to the settlement and send 'em a letter. One letter for all ten. That's the kind of boys they are. The big fight is over. From now on we'll only be discouragin' small fry."

"You didn't answer my remark, Keogh. I said you could take any or all—"

Keogh's bronzed cheeks broke before a grin, and small sun-wrinkles strayed out from his eye corners. "I'll take all, ma'am."

Night Raid

Chapter One

Night had come again, a soft desert night that damped the intolerable heat of day. In another half-hour the small campfire gleaming on the edge of the gravelly creek would be a grateful barrier against the sharp, still cold. Overhead swung the infinite canopy of heaven, its metal blue expanse shimmering with stars; far and low on the horizon the moon hung at a crazy angle, a thin-edged crescent that gave no light. A thousand miles of desert and mountain marched to this solitary outpost of man and seemed to stop, while the bark and whine of distant coyotes and the murmuring of the creek alone broke the spell of silence. Sage smell was in the air; the smell of bacon and coffee had not yet quite gone. Two horses browsed beyond the rim of light, picketed. Blankets were down, and upon them stretched two weary travelers who had ridden a good many leagues in search of rest and surcease from the carping cares of men. Indigo Bowers and Joe Breedlove camped again.

No two individuals could possibly have been more dissimilar. Indigo was short and thin; his pointed, saturnine face was homely beyond description. And as he sat humped over, staring into the flames, it appeared that he thought of all the sorrows and all the troubles the universe bequeathed its mortals. No ray of cheer broke the set pessimism of lips, no trace of humor leavened his faded blue eyes. Life, it appeared, was just one dirty trick after another. Which is to say that Indigo Bowers was in his usual frame of mind and in his usual state of health.

Joe Breedlove, on the other hand, was a tall and muscular man. The firelight gleamed along his corn-yellow hair and snapped in his hazel eyes. He was looking up—up to the stars, his body relaxed and his face mirroring the perfect serenity that was so much a part of him. Joe made friends easily, and once made these friends clove to him forever; there was a mellowness about him, a whimsicality that tempered all his acts and all his words. The world, according to Joe, was the only world available, therefore why fret?

He dropped his attention to the gloomy Indigo, fine wrinkles sprang around his temples. "Providence," said he in a voice that plucked the strings of melody, "sure thought about man's comfort when it created night an' shadows. Me, I like shadows. It's all the same as takin' a bath after a hard day's work."

Indigo emitted a rasping sound of dissent and his cigarette drooped from a corner of his thin lips. "Yeah? There you go again with that doggone romantic imagination o' yours. Seems to me Providence made night because it's ashamed o' the ant-hill it created down here. Did you ever see anything more forlorn an' useless as the country we been ridin' through lately? I'm so cussed full o' sand I grate every time I move. I'm scorched like a kernel o' popcorn. Been lookin' at sagebrush an' distance so long I got a perpetual headache."

"Well," admitted Joe, mildly reluctant, "it's a mite sparse at that, but it's sure fine grazin' land for cows."

"A cow don't know no better," argued Indigo. "Personal, I don't like this land. A self respectin' buzzard wouldn't lay an egg in it. How long we been on this so-called journey o' rest anyhow?"

"Six weeks barrin' two days," said Joe.

"Yeah, an' how much rest have we got?" Indigo grew querulous. "It's funny how folks pick on us. Nothin' but trouble, nothin' but scraps. If ever we back-track we sure will have to pick another route. Six towns in a row is layin' for our hides. Rest—huh!"

"I'm a man o' peace," drawled Joe. "I don't like to fight. If you didn't pack a temper full o' poison—"

Indigo stilled his partner with a gesture of a skinny arm and raised his somber countenance against the night. His nostrils dilated slightly, like a hound keening the wind. "They's trouble somewhere out there. I know it. Sounds to me like them coyotes is japin' us. I wish folks wouldn't pick on me."

Joe met this with a skeptical lift of eyebrows. His partner was like a bantam rooster strutting around the arena. Indigo's past life consisted of successive chapters of violence. He claimed he wanted to be left alone yet it was always noticeable that when in the proximity of a fight he grew strangely restless. It only took one small word of invitation to bring him into the tangled affairs of other people. Many men had been deceived by Indigo's wisp of a frame; when he moved, he moved like dynamite, leaving destruction in his wake. And no amount of logic ever could convince him that he was other than a mild and inoffensive creature who had been unjustly picked on. He stirred on his blanket, the washed-out blue eyes darting around the rim of light.

"Just the same, they's somethin' goin' on around here I don't like."

Joe Breedlove never moved, yet there was a slight tightening of his big frame. A sage bush rustled out beyond. Something stirred, the gravelly ground marked a body passing across the darkness, and the horses became uneasy. Both partners became unnaturally still. Out of the shadows marched a rawboned man with the russet beard of Judas and eyes that were brilliant black; a burly creature coated with dust and a general flavor about him that augured a shattering of the commandments. He squatted by the fire looking swiftly from partner to partner.

"Howdy, gents!"

"Huh," grunted Indigo, visibly annoyed. The fellow's approach violated all etiquette. Indigo believed in etiquette on the range.

"Nice evenin'," stated Joe Breedlove, mildly. "Stir

up the fire."

"I ain't cold," said the newcomer and relapsed to a full silence.

It was up to him to announce himself and the partners waited, each staring into the flames. Joe Breedlove appeared to be in a deep and profound study; the placid benevolence of his face never changed. It was otherwise with Indigo and with each passing moment he grew more and more restive until it seemed he was about to suffer an acute attack of indigestion. Then there was another sound beyond the fire's rim and a second newcomer hitched into the light and squatted by the blaze; he was built like a pole and his jaw was nearly as long as that of a horse. Once more the partners were inspected in a swift and sidling manner.

"Howdy, gents."

"The same," murmured Joe and casually draped himself in a manner that left his right arm free to swing. Indigo muttered and morosely held his peace. A moment later he flung up his head to find three other strangers marching out of the night. One by one they dropped to their haunches, none of them bothering to pass a greeting. Indigo looked across the flames to his partner, and Joe's left lid fluttered. The five visitors were as grave as redmen; the one who owned the russet beard looked around the circle and announced succinctly, "It's them all right."

"Yeah, I reckon," observed the gentleman with the horse jaw.

"You'll excuse the manner o' droppin' in," said the red-bearded gentleman to Joe and Indigo, with just a trace of deference in his words. "But we wasn't shore it was you boys. Elbow Jim is the only one which ever saw yuh an' he's laid up in town with a lot o' concussions where a hoss kicked him. I guess he's out of it for some days. Anyhow we sorter hung back an' watched yuh sashayin' acrost the country today. Elbow Jim said it'd be a big man an' a leetle man, so's we waits to get a good look."

It never took much to soothe Indigo's feelings. A sort of an apology had been offered and he accepted it with magnificent forbearance. "That's all right— that's plumb natchral."

"Well," went on the one with the red beard, "it was Elbow Jim's idea to write an' ask yuh to come down here. He had a lot o' confidence in you boys. Mebbe he told yuh all about it in the letter?"

Here was a situation. Indigo, never a great hand at deception, kept still. But Joe waved an arm. "I reckon he didn't say much. A letter, you know, is sorter public."

"That's right," agreed the red-bearded one. "Elbow'd be pretty secret. Well, it was his idea. But since he ain't here to unravel it I guess we'll have to go on without him. Me, I'm Bo Annixter. He's—" pointing to the fellow with the horse jaw, "Shirtsleeve Smith." And Bo Annixter went around the circle, calling names. The partners gravely nodded.

"The point is," proceeded this red-bearded Annixter, "we're plumb able to rustle our own critters, but lately the county's sorter tightened up. They got a sher'ff who's watchin' the railroad. We had a gent who took our stuff an' got it to market for us. Well, he

104

quit—scared out. Reckon he's made all the money he wants so he's figgerin' to be an honest gent from now on. Which leaves us up a tree."

"The country," opined Indigo, "ain't what it used to be."

"Now you said somethin'," agreed Bo Annixter. His black eyes stabbed Indigo and passed on to Joe, leaving Indigo dubious. This fellow with the red foliage looked mighty tough and so did the other four rustlers. Doggoned tough.

"That's why Elbow wrote you boys. We figgered we'd rustle the cows an' run 'em to the county line. There's where you'd take 'em an' fog 'em to yore hangout. Elbow said yuh allus had a place to sell."

"Well—" murmured Indigo and waved his arm vaguely.

"Sure—sure," interposed Annixter hastily. "We ain't askin' nothin' about yore location. Jus' take 'em an' get rid of 'em. We split fifty-fifty. That's fair enough, ain't it?"

"That's downright handsome," agreed Indigo, almost with enthusiasm.

"It ain't everybody we'd trust like that," said Annixter. "But Elbow said you was four-square gents. So that goes with us."

"Our word," declared Indigo, rearing up, "is good as gov'ment security."

All the while Joe Breedlove had maintained silence. Indigo, meeting his partner's attention, was suddenly aware that he talked too much. And, upon a

105

second observation of the five rustlers—seeing them sitting around so watchfully, and seeing the firelight slant across their hard jowls—he decided he had played the situation a little too far.

"It's like this," went on Bo Annixter, turning to Joe Breedlove. There was something about the golden-haired man that always attracted attention and respect. Inevitably he was looked upon as the leader of the pair; perhaps it was his smile, or the lazy way he carried himself, or the unbroken serenity of his countenance—at any rate when men dealt with the partners they soon came to ignore Indigo. Ordinarily Indigo would have resented such a thing, he would have risen upon his haunches and launched his defiance. But with Joe trailing beside him it was different; deep down in his heart Indigo admitted Joe to be the better head. Which was saying much for Indigo.

"It's like this," repeated Annixter. "They's the Elkhorn outfit five miles from here. Old man Stovall runs it. They's only five hands on the place. We ain't ever touched it, but now's the time. Part o' their summer range is right near the county line an' they ain't but one hand ridin' thataway. See? Shucks, it's easy. All clear?"

Joe's head bobbed slightly whereupon Indigo began to worry. He depended always on Joe to get them out of trouble—and here was Joe drifting into stormy waters.

"Fine," said Annixter, and slapped his thigh. "Then we might as well get it tonight."

Indigo bent forward to poke the fire and in so

doing got a chance to look well at his partner. Jc
appeared never so placid as now. By and by he stirred.

"How far is that Elkhorn ranch-house?" he asked,
mildly.

"Five miles due south."

More silence on Joe's part. And this very silence
plainly increased Annixter's respect. "Of course,"
said the man, "mebbe it ain't very big potatoes for
you boys. Elbow says yuh handle consid'ble beef.
Still, they's a neat profit. If yuh want, yuh can sit
right on the county line an' we'll rustle 'em to yuh."

Joe squared his shoulders. "I guess not tonight.
My partner and me always like to look a layout over
before we do business."

"Shucks, it's pie," protested Annixter, evidently
not liking the delay.

"Shore," agreed Joe. "But it's a rule of ours. Never
pays to make a pass in the dark. That's why we're still
free gents."

Annixter silently debated; the rest of the rustlers
waited. There was something so taciturn and so
calmly confident about them that Indigo, as hardy a
gentleman as he was, grew nervous. The sooner he
and Joe were out of this the better. "Yeah," said he in
a dry voice, "it's a habit o' ours."

"All right then," agreed Annixter. "We'll sleep on
it. Run over t'morra an' look. We'll do it that
evenin'."

The rustlers rose and went back into the darkness.
Saddle gear jingled, horses moved into view; and
presently the whole five were back with their
blankets, bedding down for the night. Indigo,

scratching his head, felt the sweat trickle down his cheek. And it made him mad. The fire died and the camp slumbered, though Indigo's rest was broken by the memory of Annixter's beady eyes.

At dawn the partners were up and away, leaving to Annixter and the other four the assurance that they would be back at the same rendezvous around noon. Joe was profoundly buried in one of his meditative spells and Indigo kept the silence for a good quarter of a mile, or until he looked back and saw the rustlers streaming across the land in another direction. Then he could hold himself no longer.

"Who started this doggone deception, anyhow?" he demanded.

"I'd be obliged for the information myself," said Joe, rousing. His mild glance fell upon Indigo with more than a passing interest. Indigo rose to his dignity.

"Don't look at me like that. I didn't tell 'em we was the gents they wanted to meet. Well, not exactly. Why didn't you speak up an' say it was all a mistake?"

"Why didn't you?" countered Joe, rolling himself a cigarette and studying the horizon with a far off gaze.

"I thought about it," admitted Indigo, "but judgin' from appearances it looked to me as if the news might've irritated 'em some."

"That was my conclusion likewise," agreed Joe. "And what's the use of disturbin' folks' feelin's?"

"Well," summed up Indigo, "we're supposed to be

a couple of high-class rustlers from the county to the north. Must be awful high-class, the way they trust us. An' we're supposed to be friends to this jasper Elbow Jim who's laid up with a belted coco. What gets me is how quick they figgered we was somebody we ain't. Awful careless."

"I sorter suspect," put in Joe, "that we camped on the spot the two parties was to meet. Indigo, wouldn't it be real interestin' if them two real rustlers should arrive about now, or if this gent Elbow Jim should appear on the scene?"

"I dunno," muttered Indigo in apparent despair, "why people should pick on us so. I don't see nothin' interestin' about said eventualities. All I see is a lot o' trouble. Told you so last night."

Indigo observed that Joe had a tight and familiar look upon his face. It meant profound thought and Indigo felt the chill of anticipation. It couldn't be that this easy-going partner of his— No, Joe never horned into a strange game. Still, as a kind of feeler, he put forth a general statement. "The farther we ride an' the quicker we ride the sooner we'll be out o' this mess."

"That sounds sensible," murmured Joe, still engrossed in his thoughts.

Indigo was vaguely disappointed. "Mebbe we should stop at the next town an' tell the sheriff." But in a moment he answered that for himself. "No, it wouldn't be none of our business, wouldn't it? Same as spyin'. But, say, how about droppin' into this Elkhorn outfit an' passin' a hint?"

"That ain't much different from tellin' the hounds

109

o' the law, is it? Why butt into somebody else's affairs? It's their game, not ours."

Indigo rode in moody silence for a mile before muttering, "I guess it's none of our business."

Joe had no answer for that. Indigo studied his partner surreptitiously and couldn't quite get a perverse idea out of his head that the smiling and debonair Joe was still on the rack of indecision. At the end of another ten minutes he repeated his remark. "I guess it's none of our business."

"That's right," declared Joe, as if he'd come to a decision. "We ride."

"Oh, hell!" snorted Indigo.

Joe grinned at his partner. "I thought you was tryin' to avoid any more trouble?"

"Well, but look at it," grunted Indigo. "It seems sorter stinkin' mean to me. There's that old gent who prob'ly don't deserve no misfortune. There's all them nice beeves—Joe, it don't seem right."

"Yeah, and there's all that trouble to fiddle your feet in," countered Joe. "Why don't you speak the real reason?"

Indigo refused to answer. He proceeded with a kind of smouldering excitement in his eyes and a feeling that his partner was wholly unreasonable and entirely too cautious. He knew as well as any man of the range could know that the first law was to mind his own business and not to tamper with another's quarrels unless definitely asked. Still, it seemed to him a bet was being overlooked.

*   *   *

Up from the distance rose a ranch-house surrounded by corrals and outbuildings and a scattering of cottonwoods. Joe studied the scene between half closed eyes.

"I guess," said he with admirable casualness, "we'd better drop in an' get fresh water, hadn't we?"

Indigo nodded, still resentful. They rode toward the house and presently reined in before the porch. Over the doorway spread an immense set of elkhorns. On the porch posts someone had imprinted the brand of the outfit with a hot iron—a miniature elk-horn. There was an ancient settee beside the door and in it reclined a man of about sixty with dead white hair and a florid face. He seemed quite hale and hearty, though a buffalo robe was thrown across his knees. Seeing the two partners he raised his hand by way of greeting. "Light and rest, boys."

"Why, thanks," replied Joe, eyes lingering a moment on the elkhorn brand, "but we're just passin' through. We'd trouble you, though, to show us the water. Canteens dry."

The man raised his voice, calling. "Oh, Julie!" Then he apologized. "I'd get up if I wasn't dead from the waist down. My girl will take care of you. Come from the north, eh?"

"Yeah," said Joe, only half hearing him. A girl stood in the doorway; a girl in her twenties with auburn hair and a rounding, supple body. The porch was shaded, yet it seemed to Joe Breedlove that the sunlight dwelt on her face. Gray eyes met and smiled at him.

"Julie," said the man, "take the boys' canteens an'

111

fill 'em like a good girl.''

Joe slid from the saddle, removing his hat. He collected the two canteens and passed them to the girl as if it were a ceremony. "Hate to trouble you, ma'am," he murmured, and again his voice plucked the strings of melody. Out of the saddle he made a fine showing, tall and muscular and self contained; a mature man who looked as if he loved life, who plainly had been through the world and seen it in many moods and yet could be whimsical and untouched by malice. The girl threw up her chin to study him, half grave, half smiling; just a trace of color came to her cheeks, then she retreated.

"Better stay to chuck," advised the elder man.

"It would be a command any other time," was Joe's courteous answer. "But we're just a mite rushed. Your range, I take it—your brand."

The man's chest filled. "You bet. Henry Stovall's Elkhorn ranch. Ask anybody in town about the name or the brand and see what they tell you. When I come here I used to ride herd on the Crow warriors. Long time ago. I've hired an' fired a thousand men—half of which is long dead. Now look. Four punchers and a foreman, a girl worth all of 'em and a paralyzed old duck better dead. But I bet I live to be ninety. Ain't that the way?"

"Who knows what the hole card is?" drawled Joe. "But it's tough not to be able to fork a horse."

Stovall's hands moved. "I'm a cattleman. Been one all my life. Be one after I die unless they make me shear sheep down in perdition. Does it hurt, not havin' a horse? I reckon yore man enough to know

112

the answer to that."

"Well, you can still smell the wind," was Joe's grave answer, "an' hear the beaver-tails bellerin' out in the brakes. That's somethin'."

Around the corner of the house rolled a young man with dust on his chubby face. He was hatless and jet black hair curled around his head. Responsibility seemed to rest heavily on his mind, for he was very grave and he studied the partners with a quick, measured glance. Joe, who was a good hand at judging his own kind, decided that this chap was competent even if he wasn't much beyond voting age; and he returned the short nod with an amicable jerk of his own head.

"That calico is busted to work," said the youngster, to Stovall. "But he won't never be worth a whole lot."

"Let it lay," replied Stovall. "You boys are all a little heavy-handed with the ridin' stock. Takes an old-timer to deal with the cayuses." He turned his attention toward the partners again. "I could use some experienced hands. Want a job?"

"What for?" interposed the young man with just a trace of belligerence. "Ain't we got enough men already, considerin' everything?"

Stovall spoke soothingly. "All right, Slip. I know you're the foreman an' it's your place to hire an' fire. But I like old heads around me an' I ain't had none for a powerful long time. I'm repeatin'—there's a job for both you boys."

The girl came out with the canteens, in time to hear her father offer the partners work. A kind of alertness crossed her face, a touch of expectancy. Joe took the canteens and entirely by accident his big paw brushed her white hand. Thus they returned steady inspections until Joe dropped his head, smiling. "I'm obliged," said he and moved to his pony. Slip, the foreman, was still young enough not to be able to conceal jealousy; his lips tightened, he was not far removed from sullenness.

Joe climbed to the saddle; his eyes looked to the spreading elkhorns and again to the girl. "Thank you kindly, sir. But we've already got employment. We'll be ridin'."

The foreman disappeared back of the house. Joe and Indigo rode off. A hundred yards removed the tall partner turned in the saddle and raised his hand as a farewell. The girl still stood on the porch and her arm came up in reply.

All this while Indigo had said nothing. In company he seldom spoke, he always felt ill at ease and willing to have the more polished Joe take care of the amenities. But he missed nothing, he thoroughly inventoried the ranch and its state of prosperity in the few moments they had been by the porch. And he also had observed the glance the girl bestowed upon Joe. Well, many men admired Joe—and some women. How could it be otherwise? He turned to his partner and discovered that Joe was studying him quite soberly.

"News to me we had a job," grunted Indigo.

"I guess—" began Joe, and thereupon stopped.

The youthful foreman came spurring toward them. The partners halted and waited till he came up.

"Didn't aim to be unsociable back there," he explained, still a little surly. "But the old man is losin' his grip. Think's he's better off than he really is. Always wants to hire somebody. You savvy, I guess."

"Sho'," murmured Joe.

Indigo got the idea these two fellows were sparring with each other; the foreman was measuring Joe and Joe in turn seemed to be reading the foreman. The silence was broken by the youth.

"See any tracks north of here?"

"What kind of tracks?" drawled Joe.

"I'd guess you know what kind of tracks I'm meanin'," replied the foreman significantly.

"We're only strangers passin' through," observed Joe in a curiously soft voice.

"Then you wouldn't know what's goin' on in this county," said the foreman. With no more parley he wheeled and rode off. The partners went on until the ranch buildings were lost below the undulating ground. Then, as if both were animated by the same idea, they came to a stop.

"Well, Indigo."

"Well?"

"You know blamed well we can't go an' squeal to the sher'ff," said Joe with a trace of impatience. "We ain't built that way."

"Didn't say we was, did I?"

"An' it'd be the same if we tried to tell those folks at the ranch, wouldn't it? We don' play double."

"You say it," grunted Indigo, not able to fathom his partner's intentions.

"I guess we better sashay back to the beetle-faced gents an' see this through."

"Yeah?" snorted Indigo. "So we should turn rustlers. Then what?"

"Well, if they rustle the critters in the dark and turn 'em over to us, we can throw the stock right back on the Elkhorn range can't we? Nobody's the wiser for the time bein'. Then we pull stakes and get out of this country. By then the real pair o' rustlers from the north will show up an' Annixter's gang will realize they've spilled the beans. They'll shy off from poachin' on Elkhorn again, figgerin' the ranch will be warned. And meanwhile the Elkhorn riders'll see all them tracks on their territory an' keep strict watch. Don't it work out? Nobody's hurt by the transaction an' we won't be squealin'. Leaves our conscience plumb clean."

The distinction was somewhat too fine for Indigo's forthright soul. He said as much, adding, "Supposin' the real pair is on deck when we go back? Or supposin' this gent Elbow Jim has showed up?"

"All we need is today an' tonight. It's a gamble we got to take."

"I dunno why it is you always got to do things the hard way," muttered Indigo. "Always got to embroider an' hemstitch till we're up to our neck in the soup."

"Great Caesar, wasn't you the fellow who wanted

116

rouble a minute ago?" inquired Joe.

"In moderation," was Indigo's reply. "I want a run or my money. This is jus' foolish. Nothin' but alamity can come of it."

"Well then, we'll keep headin' south an' forget it," lecided Joe.

"Oh, hell, didn't I say I was willin'?" snapped ndigo. "Let's go. But jus' remember we're turnin' llegal. Don't forget it none. Mebbe we got good ntentions but when we're caught nobody's goin' to now it. I don't see nothin' but sorrow. Well, if we ot to do it, then we got to. Come on."

They described a wide circle in the prairie and truck north toward the rendezvous with Annixter nd his rustlers. Joe Breedlove was as serene and enevolent as the winds of May; Indigo's pale blue yes took on a certain narrowed fixity. The both of hem were riding into action and each accepted the act with characteristic expressions.

Chapter Two

When the partners, thoughtful and somewhat wary, reached the meeting place by the creek, Annixter's gang had not yet returned, and for this breathing spell both Joe and Indigo were thankful. The sun stood at its high mark; being normal men they were hungry, so they boiled a little coffee, fried some bacon and rummaged cold biscuits out of their rolls. After that they smoked in the shade of the cottonwoods, seeming drowsy yet not for an instant relaxing from a constant scrutiny of the horizon. They meant, above all else, to see the rustlers approaching in time enough to count noses. The sun slid west and the afternoon droned along.

"The beetle-eyed jasper," muttered Indigo, "said we didn't have to do any actual rustlin'. Said we could wait on the county line an' he'd bring the critters to us. Sounds reasonable to me."

"That won't work," argued Joe. "We've got to know where they get said cows else we won't know where to take 'em back."

"Was you aimin' to set each brute in its identical tracks?" questioned Indigo, scornfully. "Joe, I never mistrust yore abilities, but I shore do know you've got an awful habit o' addin' a lot o' unnecessary fancy work to an ordinary chore."

"The closer we stay to those fellows from now to midnight the safer we'll be," returned Joe. "We got a responsibility and we might as well see it through proper."

"Yeah, you're always hell for proper," grumbled Indigo. "Wish I had more cartridges."

"Dust off to the east," announced Joe.

The partners rose up in unison and stationed themselves at no great distance from the waiting horses. The dust cloud grew, and presently riders spurred through it into sight. Indigo squinted long and carefully.

"One more thing," murmured Joe, the words tightening, "in case of trouble and in case it's each fellow for himself, hit for those bluffs toward the northeast there."

"Then," snapped Indigo, rising to his full five feet, five inches, "we'd better hit pronto. They was only five gents last night an' right now they's six. Bet it's that Elbow Jim jasper. What about it?"

Joe looked for himself. Six riders came along at a lope, side by side, rising and falling in unison. The partners swapped somber glances and moved toward their horses. Presently they were a-saddle, yet they tarried.

"No use runnin'," grunted Indigo. "I don't feel

crooked enough to let a bunch o' mugs like them chase me."

"Make it two," murmured Joe. He had a small, set smile on his face; and as the party swung into the grove his arm hung free beside his gun. Indigo appeared to have another severe attack of indigestion; his homely, wizened features were twisted at odd angles and the light of battle flickered in his blue eyes, turning them to a queer shade of green. Annixter, foremost, flung up an arm and the group halted. The sixth man, both partners were quick to note, was a shackling gentleman with a fever and ague face. He sat crooked over as if he were saddle galled, his clothes were wrinkled and one side of his head was wrapped in a blue neck piece. Undeniably this was Elbow Jim, and Elbow Jim at the present moment looked toward the partners with a vacant, unknowing glance.

Annixter slid to the ground, speaking to Joe. "Elbow, the damned fool, wouldn't stay in his bunk. Had to come along. No use tellin' him anything, but he'll croak for it yet."

Joe was the picture of laziness. "Hello there, Elbow."

Elbow Jim seemed to be startled. He focused his attention, much as a man might strive to see through a fog. "Who are you?" he growled.

Annixter, shielded by his horse, tapped his head with a finger and winked at Breedlove.

"Shucks," protested Joe, still talking to Elbow,

'don't you know yore old friends? Remember the time—"

"Who are you?" demanded Elbow. "What's all this foolishness about? I don't know yuh atall."

Annixter spoke up. "It's the boys you wrote to up north, Elbow. They come down, like you asked. We're all set now."

"No, we ain't set," contradicted Elbow Jim. "Never laid eyes on either party. It's a frame-up."

Elbow spoke with energy; the tone carried conviction. Annixter's head reared and his sparkling black eyes flashed from partner to partner, narrowing and hardening. The rest of the rustlers sat like ramrods in the saddles. Indigo, never a man to endure suspense any length of time, broke in angrily.

"What's the matter with you, anyhow? Ain't you got good sense?"

"What's yore monnickers?" asked Elbow craftily.

"My name?" snorted Indigo. And by the way he weaved in the saddle, Joe knew his partner was about to fling down the gage of battle. "If anybody around these premises wants to hear my name it's—"

"Hold on," interrupted Joe. He leaned toward Elbow and spoke persuasively. "Now, Elbow, don't you remember the night in the Dollarhide Saloon?"

Joe had seen that saloon in the course of their trip southward. It happened to be in the town that was the seat of the county to the north—that county in which he and Indigo were supposed to do their rustling. And since Elbow Jim was a friend of these two unknown rustlers it stood to reason he must have met them on their own territory and possibly in that very saloon. It was a chance shot in the dark. Elbow obviously struggled with his reason. He had been badly battered on the head and most of his faculties jarred out of him. "Don't you remember that, Elbow?" repeated Joe, in the tone of one talking to a backward child.

Of a sudden Elbow dropped from his horse and walked away. "My God, what's all this? Am I bugs? My haid hurts."

There had been a faint trace of suspicion in Annixter's eyes, but this last moment seemed to dispel it. He came toward the partners, lowering his voice. "No wonder his coco hurts. They's a dent in it big enough to sink an aig. Reckon he's off the track for keeps. Ain't been talkin' straight since he got kicked."

"Looks some thinner to me," observed Joe with an air of considered judgment.

Annixter nodded, thinking of other things. "Well, how about it? See what you want to see this mornin'?"

"I reckon," agreed Joe. "Any time you say."

Annixter's shoulders rose, his jaws closed like a trap. "Fine! It's three hours to dusk. We travel then."

In that gloaming hour when dusk marched out of the horizons and the cobalt shadows piled thicker over the land the party swung to horse and turned due east. They traveled silently and swiftly for a half mile, Annixter in the lead, Elbow Jim alongside. The injured rustler kept mumbling to himself, turning a puzzled eye on the partners. And finally he stopped, bringing the cavalcade to a halt with him.

"I'm goin' back," he announced.

"What for?" demanded Annixter, showing impatience. "Don't gum up the works, Elbow. We got business on hand an' it ain't like you to lag."

"I'm going back," repeated Elbow Jim stubbornly. "Seems like I remember I was to meet some fellows by the crick. It seems like I was."

"Why, you darned fool, here they are, right with us," reasoned Annixter.

But Elbow Jim shook his head. "They ain't the ones. Seems like I was to meet somebody." And without any more argument he left them and rode away. Annixter's head dropped, he stared at the ground for quite a spell. By and by he looked to the partners and in the interval it seemed as if he fought with his suspicions. Indigo's eyes, not visible to the rest of the party in the shadows, turned green again; Joe was relaxed and casual, though his attention never wavered from the leader.

"Maybe," he suggested, "I better go round him up."

"Let him mosey," decided Annixter. "He ain't much help anyhow." His hard glance measured Joe and fell away. "We ride."

They went on into the deepening night, hoofs drumming the ground. A small wind sprang up, the heat of day vanished. Once more the stars were out and the moon hung lifeless on the world's rim. Annixter kept a steady course into the east for an hour, then gradually veered south, checking the gait

123

imperceptibly with the passing minutes. Joe judged that they were at a far corner of the Elkhorn range, traveling away from the ranch buildings all the while. It also seemed to him Annixter was circling toward his objective, not going in a straight line. Annixter, he decided, was a capable hombre and one who easily assumed authority. Certain it was the rest of the rustlers obeyed him without a murmur of dissent; a hard, unscrupulous fellow who would put a good front on anything he did. Joe's experience with lawless gentry was wide and varied; most of them were braggarts and bullies, with a courage that faded in a showdown. He rated Annixter as being of tougher grain. An inner warning bothered him; Annixter's bulky body made a formidable shadow in the darkness.

The leader grunted, and the group came to a halt. Annixter spoke in a rumbling undertone. "All right, Shirtsleeve."

Shirtsleeve Smith proceeded on alone. Annixter touched Joe's arm. "Ain't far now. When we round the brutes we hit direct north into them buttes. They's a pass thataway we go through. County line beyond. It's yore play then. I guess you know the country over there?"

"Yeah."

"How long will it take you boys to polish off the deal?"

Joe answered easily. "Three days."

Annixter seemed to be surprised. "That's pretty sudden."

"We do it sudden," responded Joe. "No use havin'

llegal beef around you any longer'n necessary. It's he reason we're still out o' jail."

"Elbow thinks a lot o' you boys," said Annixter. Joe caught a trailing doubt in the words, but he forebore answering. Shirtsleeve Smith's shadow returned.

"All clear."

"We ride," grunted Annixter.

They traveled slower this time, the ponies' hoofs making a small and sibilant confusion in the sand. Within fifteen minutes they stopped again. Cattle ahead, cattle smell in the air and the vague outline of their presence. Annixter spoke. "All right, Shirtsleeve—Red—Mac."

The indicated ones left the group and merged with the velvet pall. The warning in Joe's head grew clearer and more insistent. This Annixter party did things too competently. No fuss, no excitement. It was like a drill. Too smooth, too doggoned smooth. Probably Annixter had a lot of other plans concealed behind that red foliage—for instance, in case he decided there was trickery in the partners' presence. Running those critters back to their original range wasn't going to be half as easy as it seemed.

Cattle moved slowly. Annixter's voice was slightly brittle. "Go ahead, Buck."

The rustler remaining with Annixter rode away, heading toward the Elkhorn ranch buildings. "Allus keep a man on our tail to watch for trouble," murmured Annixter.

Joe feigned a hearty approval. "I shore like yore

style, Annixter. Wish you was with us boys up north."

"It's an idea," grunted Annixter. The man was human enough to be flattered. "This country's gettin' washed out. They's a sher'ff who's hell on wheels. Elbow won't never be good no more. An' we're gettin' too prominent in the county. Said sheriff was elected on a promise to clean us out an' the fool actually figgers to do it. Well, here we are."

Cattle moved by them at a shambling, uneasy pace. Soft oaths broke the night, and the slap of quirts. Annixter and the partners fell in behind. Joe assumed a sudden authority. "Lay on 'em now. We've got to mosey."

Annixter mildly protested. "What's the rush? This is easy."

"My style," replied Joe a little more crisply. "Didn't I say we worked fast?"

The pace increased; Annixter sidled off and was gone for some time, during which interval Indigo edged closer to his partner and started to speak. Joe interrupted with a quick phrase. "Neat work, ain't it Indigo? I like these boys' style." And Indigo, warned, held his tongue. A rider drew up to them, coming from some unexpected angle, and rode between, never saying a word. Annixter returned, also silent. The mass of shadow that was the rustled stock weaved uncertainly. Hoofs and horns clacked; the pound and shuffle of their gallop rose into the night.

"Shirtsleeve—drop back," snapped Annixter. And the man riding between the partners faded and was lost. "We're leavin' a broad trail. But they was an Elkorn rider makin' the circle this mornin' an' I doubt f he'll get around till late tomorrow. That's ample ime for you boys?"

"Plenty," said Joe.

"We'll meet yuh four days from now at the crick," uggested Annixter. But Joe knew that was more of a equest than a suggestion. Annixter seemed to grow nore gruff as the night wore along; more distant.

"Agreed," was Joe's response.

After an hour the ground began to grow rougher and he outline of the broken country stood up before hem. Annixter disappeared again. When he re- urned Joe felt the stock turning to another point of he compass. They dipped down and up several arroyos, they passed a clump of jackpines. On they nurried. The slope grew steeper, it turned rocky underfoot, the pace slackened and the horses began to breathe harder.

"The pass," said Annixter and for the third time rode off. The cattle were at a walk. High ground stretched on either side and the walls of a small canyon narrowed on them, pinching the whole pro- cession to a long, trickling line. There were trees up this way, the breeze scoured against them, fresh and cold. Riders lagged and fell in behind. Then they were going up a stiff grade—a grade that of a sudden dropped into a summit meadow. The trees marched out to them, surrounded them; a coyote barked, the party came to a halt.

"Your turn, I reckon," said Annixter, returning.

"Down the far slope is the county line."

Joe took off his Stetson and dropped his watch into it. Then he lit a match and discovered it was even twelve. All this had taken longer than it seemed; dawn wasn't more than four hours removed—four hours in which to undo all that had been done. "All right," said he.

"Don't let this rough country fool yuh," warned Annixter. "Bear due north. Either way from that'll push yuh into a lot o' blind pockets. I'd go on straight to the line, but it's better we go back an' make a lot o' tracks leadin' another direction. One o' the gang, howsumever, will keep a lookout around these parts after daylight. If he sees anybody comin' afore yuh get far enough off he'll send up a smoke signal. Watch yore back trail for that."

"Good enough," murmured Joe. The rustlers had collected, waiting for Annixter to finish. The man tarried, saying nothing at all, yet bending close to Joe. Joe saw only a blur of Annixter's face; then the leader withdrew.

"Four days from tonight, at the creek," he called.

"That's right," agreed Joe. *"Adios."*

The rustlers dipped down the grade and presently the partners, listening carefully, lost the sound of them. Indigo sighed, as if he were pulling himself up by the roots. "Well, we got somethin' on our—"

Joe's arm touched him. "Easy, Indigo. Hold it a minute."

They waited five minutes longer, but nothing stirred the profound stillness of this night save the slight and uneasy movement of the stock. Joe stirred and spoke in a matter of fact voice, slightly louder than appeared necessary. "All right, now we've got to drive 'em hard as long as it's dark. Let's push 'em."

They pressed against the rear of the cattle. Indigo rode around to edge in the flanks. Once more the momentum of the mass carried the small herd along the trail and across the level ground of the diminutive meadow. Under cover of this orderly confusion Joe closed upon Indigo and spoke just above a whisper. "Keep 'em going five-ten minutes, Indigo. I'm waitin' on the trail. Think somebody's apt to be followin' us."

He left his horse at the side of the trail, back in the pines, and retraced his way afoot for a hundred yards. Here he stopped and waited. The noise of the cattle came to him as a muffled echo. Elsewhere was no movement save the slight scouring of the wind in the pine tops.

"Somethin' bothered that Annixter gent," he said to himself. "He's a shrewd duck. Think maybe he'd have a man track us till we got out o' the county, jus' to find if we was up to specifications."

He drew back a yard or so. A horse came up the slope, picking its way cautiously and with only the slight shuffle of its hoofs and the small abrasion of saddle leather to announce it. Well, there wasn't need for much caution; the noise of the herd would drown out this kind of pursuit. That fellow Annixter was nobody's fool, he took care of all bets. Joe's arm dropped toward his gun and he retreated still farther.

129

The rider was muttering sibilantly to his animal. "Get along—get along. Don't yuh know cow smell?" Man and beast were abreast of Joe. Joe tarried one more instant; then his tall body weaved across the space and came up somewhat behind the rider. His arms swept forward and all his strength snapped into them. The horse reared. Down out of the saddle came the rider, fighting. A bellow woke the echoes as he hit the ground. Joe struck him on the face with a driving blow and his gun touched the man's ribs. "Easy, brother. Make it easy." There was a quick turning and slashing of legs and arms, a subdued volley of oaths. Joe's gun barrel laid along the fellow's head and then resistance died. The herd, evidently had stopped for Joe couldn't make out their progress; but Indigo was coming back at the gallop.

"All right. Draw in, Indigo. I got a nibble. Bring me yore rope."

Indigo groped toward Joe. "He's out? Lessee his complexion, Joe. An' do yuh reckon the rest o' that gang heard the yelp he lets loose."

"Don't believe so. They left him behind to scout. I figger they're well on the way to the crick by now. Light a match."

Yellow light sputtered under the protection of Indigo's extended hat-brim and the flickering rays fell upon the horse-jawed Shirtsleeve Smith. Shirtsleeve was unconscious and unlovely. The light sputtered out; Indigo wasted no time with his lariat, nor did he waste gentleness as he looped and knotted the cord about the recumbent rustler. Joe started to untie the man's bandanna and fashion a gag but

130

Indigo, catching on to the operation, interrupted. "Lemme do that. You can palaver a whole lot better'n me, but when it comes to such chores as these here I'm the golden haired lad. If yuh want to know the positive truth, Joe, that feller Annixter reminds me o' bad medicine."

"Make it two."

The partners boosted the still mentally absent Shirtsleeve Smith to his feet and carried him back through the pines to a spot that felt secluded from the open ground. Then they retraced their way toward the herd. "Good thing them brutes is tired or they'd be scattered from hell to supper. Joe, I ain't no saint, but it gripes me to be an amachoor rustler. Tain't a matter of morals either. It's a matter o' legal impediments. To state the bald facts it's a matter o' a knot under one ear."

"We've got less than four hours, Indigo. Have to hustle this."

"Why not run 'em anywhere down into the flat country an' leave 'em. That's near enough ain't it?"

"Not by five miles it ain't, Indigo. Supposin' Annixter should be ridin' this way at daylight an' see 'em all ready to be pushed back up here out of sight. He'd do just that. And there'd be our good intentions shore shot to pieces."

Indigo grunted. "You're just doin' fancy work now an' you know it. Yuh just got an idea an' yuh won't let go."

"Put it like that," agreed Joe. "Let's mosey."

*   *   *

131

They circled the cows and milled them back upon the trail, traveling across the meadow and down the slope. Presently they were on level ground again, urging the brutes to a gallop. They had no exact idea as to where the main part of the Elkhorn herd ranged, but being old and experienced at night riding they did know the approximate direction and the approximate distance back along the route. About an hour and a half of this progress would bring them to a good enough destination. Another hour and a half would put them well out of the way—just as dawn arrived. Not exactly a comfortable margin, but still sufficient if they kept fogging on during the day.

Joe looked up to the dim stars and grinned wryly. Well, maybe Indigo was right. It was a stubborn idea, this of running the brutes back to where they originally had been. It needn't be so close, almost anywheres along here was really good enough. But Joe Breedlove, as mild and peaceable man as he was, had queer streaks of illogical sentiment in him. He loved, above all else, to put an adequate and artistic end to his chores. Indigo, now, was more of a realist. When the small and wizened one got into a jackpot his method was to drive ahead and tap somebody on the coco. That was effective, but to Joe it wasn't satisfactory. Joe's method was to use his silver tongue; if that failed then he resorted to stratagem, tied his man and lectured the unfortunate on philosophy.

In the present case there happened to be another motive. Up among those stars was the face of a girl—the clear and rounding face of Julie Stovall—with her auburn hair and her gray eyes. She had looked at him with favor, there had been something of understanding in the short, grave glance. It reminded Joe of earlier days, of a time when he was a stripling and his future seemed to be settled among quiet ways. Well, that had gone under the bridge. But though time softened and mellowed the disappointment, it only took such a woman's look to unlock Joe's treasure box of memories. And then Joe's smile became a little wry and the magnificent chivalry of the man flamed high. As tonight.

Out of the darkness came a tremor of sound that was above and beyond the rumble of hoofs. Indigo had heard it too for he came in from a flank muttering.

"Hear that, Joe?"

Joe bent his head and listened. It vanished, then it came again, more strongly. Indigo grumbled. "To the right of us. Listen, we're makin' enough noise to wake the dead."

"Let the brutes run on a ways," murmured Joe. "We'll stick here."

"I'd jus' as soon orphan them cows right now."

"Easy, Indigo. Sift to the left some. You'd think the whole county was out ridin' tonight." His voice trailed to a mere whisper. "Sift. They ain't far away."

The cattle galloped on a piece then, no longer pressed, broke the pace and split in twenty different directions. Joe Breedlove saw the compact shadow of them dissolve and disappear. They were all over the compass. He heard Indigo shift restlessly in the saddle. Elsewhere was the sound of somebody circling and advancing. Elkhorn outfit—posse—

133

rustlers? Joe didn't know, but any of the three possibilities spelled poison for he and Indigo. It was hell to be honest tonight, and it was hell to be crooked. However, the straying cows shielded them somewhat.

"Never get 'em together again," he thought to himself. "Looks as if we leave 'em here and fog."

The outline of horse and rider moved in. Behind was the clink of a bridle chain. There was more than one and they were quietly prospecting the area, quietly dragging back and forth. Joe felt a presence to his left hand and he drew himself up, his head sweeping from side to side. Best to freeze until these gents got tired and passed by. If it happened to be Annixter's party a little lead slinging wouldn't hurt, but if it were either Elkhorn men or a posse the less gun play the better.

Indigo couldn't keep from stirring. Joe put out his arm to touch him in warning. At that moment Indigo's horse, smelling his own kind, elected to whinny. Suddenly riders drove toward the partners from all angles and there was a slapping and a jingling of gear and a challenging of voices.

"That's them! Bear down!"

Annixter's men!

"Out of this," muttered Joe, turning his horse. "Back to the buttes. Come on, Indigo, don't get reckless."

But Indigo had labored and sweated hard enough for his fun and now he meant to satisfy his ingrained instinct for trouble. Joe saw the little man rear in the stirrups; Indigo's cracked, falsetto tones sheered the night in ribald defiance. "Yuh suckers, come an' collect!"

Annixter's voice, hard and crisp seemed to carry over their heads. "Draw off, Mac." And at that somebody at their rear spurred away. Then the tornado struck. Mushrooming points of light glowed, flat waves of sound spat in their faces. They were whipsawed. Indigo's gun roared, the wizened one swayed in his saddle like a common drunk and he yelled again. "What smells around here? Polecats!" Joe, who fought more methodically sent a brace of bullets toward a gun flash on his flank. Annixter shouldn't have more than four men, for Shirtsleeve Smith was tied and cached up in the pines. But in spite of that the rustler leader had found help somewhere; he could tell it from the revolver echoes. Must be six in the bunch. And they were whirling around like raiding Indians. Joe made up his mind on the spot.

"Come on, Indigo. Shells cost money an' dead is a long time."

They reined about and raced away. For a moment the volleying diminished; then they heard Annixter's gang in full pursuit. The protection of the buttes was about a half hour off, or less and the shadows were blacker—that piling up of shadows that came just before first dawn. The sharp wind struck their cheeks, the stars were dim. On they plunged.

It seemed to Joe that they gained distance. All firing ceased for a little while and there was only the pound of their own animals beneath them. But, some

135

minutes later, Joe's ears caught the echo of the trailing rustlers again and for the next quarter hour the partners laid on their quirts with the knowledge they were but a scant hundred yards ahead of catastrophe. Presently they reached the rougher ground and Joe veered a little. "Hear 'em, Indigo?"

"Nope."

"Neither do I. They ain't direct behind any more. Damn that Annixter gent. He's as slick as a boiled onion."

"Their hosses is about as tired as ours, Joe. An' they can't be exactly shore which direction we take."

"That ain't the answer," grunted Joe. "They got somethin' up their elbows."

"Well, there's the end o' a good deed which never got done," muttered Indigo. "I wasn't so cracked about this business o' foggin' them critters clear back. But now that them dudes have spoiled our little journey I'm all in favor o' seein' it clear through."

"We ain't finished yet," Joe replied. "We'll hole up in the timber an' think about it."

They struck the entrance to the pass, wound in and around the rugged slopes and arrived at the narrowing walls once more. At that point disaster overtook them. Hemmed on either flank they were arrested by Annixter's harsh and peremptory order rolling down from the fore. "You're boxed. Stop right there!"

"Not me!" cried Indigo and sank his spurs. The partners flung themselves onward. The defile rang like a forge, bullets whipped at them from front and rear. Joe felt the shock of Indigo's horse colliding against his own pony and the succeeding moment

Indigo was calling up from the ground. "They plugged my brute, Joe. Go on, beat it!"

Annixter sang at them again. "Throw yore guns thisaway!"

Joe slid from the saddle and retreated to his partner. The rustlers pressed nearer from either direction, barely outlined in the dim morning's dusk. Well, they could make a fight of it yet, but what was the use of the extra killing? Annixter had only to draw back, post guards, and wait for daylight. Meanwhile here he and Indigo were, exposed to the crossfire. This was the end of one episode; tomorrow was another day.

"All right," he muttered, "we're through."

Indigo swore like a man in pain, but Joe touched his partner's arm, whispering. "Remember what we decided once, old timer."

"Stop that parleyin'!" boomed Annixter. "Throw yore guns thisaway or we'll open up!"

The partners obeyed. Annixter's men crept along cautiously and in a moment Joe and Indigo were prisoners. Light wavered across the eastern horizon.

Chapter Three

Immediately after the partners were disarmed and both tied into Joe's saddle, Annixter left a single man to guard them and withdrew down the slope a few yards to hold a parley. There seemed to be a division of opinion in the party, a heated contest between caution and recklessness in which the leader lost ground. At first nothing but the general sound of their talk reached Joe and Indigo, but as the discussion grew warmer they caught what went on.

"Daylight's about here," said Annixter. "They'll be an Elkhorn man ridin' circle. Why not wait till dark?"

"By which time said gent will see all them tracks an' then the whole danged ranch will be on the scout. If we git 'em, we got to git 'em now."

"They'll shore trail us then," argued Annixter.

"What of it? Ain't these hills big enough to cache in till dark? Then we can slip the stuff on across the line."

"It's a big risk," grumbled Annixter. "Don't you

boys reco'nize the fact we got to live in this section? You're out of it—we ain't."

"Risk either way. We come a hell of a long distance on Elbow's call an' we can't stew aroun' here for a week while the excitement simmers down. If we wait another day to git them brutes we're only lettin' them folks fix a nice trap. If we go round 'em up now we can choose our own country to fight in—if we got to fight."

"I don't like it," protested Annixter. After this followed a flurry of argument. Joe understood then the situation. The pair of real rustlers from the north had arrived and Annixter's party had fallen in with them. A silence came over the group, broken finally by the leader's reluctant assent. "All right. We'll go do it. But I got to leave a man out there today to take care of the Elkhorn line rider. Can't have him discover tracks an' run for help before we git everything settled an' out o' the way."

"We'll hide the critters up in the timber until dark," said one of the northerners. "Then we fog back with 'em. Shucks, what you afraid of?"

"Talk's cheap and it don't buy no ribbons," muttered Annixter. He returned to the partners. "What'd you highbinders do with Shirtsleeve?"

"Up in the brush takin' a wink," drawled Joe.

Annixter accepted this with an ominous mildness. "It's the fool's own fault for not bein' more careful. Well, I give it to you boys for bein' slick. We'll count up the marbles later. Elbow, come here."

The figure of Elbow Jim appeared through the filmy shadows. "Yeah?"

"You tail these fellows back into where that big

cedar is. An' don't have no lapse o' memory either."

"Don't worry," mumbled Elbow. "I ain't all finished."

Annixter retreated, the whole party rode down the trail. Elbow grunted at his prisoners. "Mosey up. I may be crazy, but I know a face when I see it. Go 'long."

The horse carrying both partners moved up the trail and back to the small meadow. It was light enough now to distinguish the beaten pathway and the occasional stumps and boulders.

"Turn left," said Elbow, and circled the partners' horse to swing it off the trail into a lesser and much overgrown trace. This led them through ever thickening underbrush, down steep slopes and along miniature canyons. From the prairie this mass of buttes had not seemed large, but now that they were away from the open country everything took on greater proportions. It was a good place to hide in or be lost in. Apparently the pass cut across the most gentle part of the ridge for the longer they traveled the more they climbed and twisted; once they had sight of a waterfall spraying against sheet rock a hundred feet below. Then they were more thoroughly enmeshed in the pines and the clinging brush.

"Turn left," droned Elbow, and again rode in to press the partners' pony. They broke through what seemed a wall of trees and came out in a glade not more than fifteen feet across. Elbow stopped and got down. Daylight flooded down, dew sparkled on

140

the grass.

"This," said Joe in genuine appreciation, "is shore pretty ain't it?"

"Nice place for a murder," was Indigo's gloomy response. "Say, fella, you goin' to keep us up on this barbecue platform much longer?"

Elbow circled the pair, looking out from under his shaggy brows with a sly shrewdness. "No tricks, no tricks on pore ol' Elbow. I may be cracked but it don't hurt my shootin' none."

"Tricks with what?" snorted Indigo. "I can't do nothin' but google my eyes."

Elbow came over and cut the ropes fastening the partners to the saddle. "Git down—march over an' sit agin that log. No—not so clos't together. Yuh might fiddle with t'other's wrist hobbles. Ol' Elbow's still got a lick of sense."

The partners with their hands tightly lashed behind them, sat against the designated log and held their peace. Elbow roamed the small glade impatiently, his head turning to odd angles and every now and then he murmured a garbled phrase to himself. Anything interested him, many objects puzzled him. Once he stooped to the ground and was thus hunched over for a matter of minutes. Then he came toward the partners and swept them with the same sly look they had observed before. The longer he watched the more uneasy he grew, until at last he spoke.

"I don't know you gents."

"Why of course you do," said Joe soothingly. "We've hoisted many a glass at the Dollarhide."

Elbow Jim wrinkled his nose and peered down it

141

somberly. "Ol' Elbow's shore cracked. Once, by Gabriel, there wasn't a man in the county what was able to down me. This was my gang, yuh hear me? Bo Annixter's boss now. Oh, Bo's all right, but he couldn't hold a candle to me. Them dam' hosses."

"Remember the Dollarhide?" persisted Joe.

"I know what I know," mumbled Elbow Jim, and he looked very shrewd.

Joe studied the log casually. "I'm sorter uncomfortable here, Elbow. It's a poor way to treat an old friend like me. But of course you got orders from Annixter an' I reckon you got to obey 'em—"

"Once I didn't," was Elbow Jim's quick reply. "But I'm out of it now. Yuh don't know Annixter like me. When he's got the bulge he keeps it. I'm kinder sorry for you gents. How'd you git in this scrape?"

He seemed to have lucid moments, moments in which he understood what had taken place. Then quite of a sudden his mind went off the track and he was both puzzled and sly, forgetting what he had said the instant previously. Joe went on. "I'm sittin' on a rock. Got any objections if I move over a little."

"Jus' so's yuh don't git nearer the skinny feller," agreed Elbow Jim.

Joe moved himself in a series of crow-hopping jumps, back all the while touching the log. Indigo's semi-closed eyes flickered with a baleful green light and he utilized Elbow's averted attention to do something with his pinioned hands. Joe's progress put the

142

partners farther apart and made it more difficult for Elbow to keep them within the range of a single glance; nor did Elbow notice that when Joe stopped and leaned on the log he had his back directly against an out-thrust knot with a splintered edge. Joe timed this well. Elbow moved around the glade with a sorry jaded expression on his battered face. The man was in bad shape; fresh blood caked the bandanna on his head.

Joe's body went rigid with effort and his arms snapped powerfully and fell limp as Elbow faced the partners again. "Yuh dunno Annixter. What he's got he keeps. Who're you boys? I'm cracked all right, but I know what I know."

After that he resumed his moody tramping, head swinging with his feet, gun dangling loosely in his fist. The morning wore along, the sun marched upward in the sky, the glade was flooded with a bright hot light. The partners seemed to accept their situation, attempting no more talk; but in those odd intervals when Elbow's attention left them Joe's arms bent outward, twisted and flexed. Beads of sweat crusted his forehead, stolidness touched his eyes—a sure sign that Joe was torturing himself.

It was more than an hour—nearer two hours since they had been captured—when they heard a voice sounding far through the trees. Elbow turned his back to the partners and cocked his head. Indigo stirred and looked warningly to Joe; the latter nodded grimly.

"Elbow," he purred, "be a good gent an' roll me a cigareet. Seems like you'd ought to treat an old friend like me better'n this."

Elbow holstered his gun. "I been in the Dollar-hide all right." He holstered his gun and went searching for tobacco and papers. Brush rustled nearer, somebody swore. Elbow rolled the cigarette with a tantalizing slowness, so slowly that Indigo began to squirm restlessly and Joe struggled to keep a serene countenance. Elbow shambled across the space, the cigarette between outstretched thumb and forefinger. "No monkey business," he warned Joe. "I ain't to be took in nobody's camp. Open yore mouth."

He was within a yard of Joe. The latter tilted his shoulders forward, he had his feet crossed beneath him. As Elbow took the next step Indigo suddenly called out, "Say, Elbow, what's this over here—"

The trick was about to work. Elbow swung. Yet the spring Joe was on the point of making, never materialized; the impulse, swiftly checked, almost carried him over on his face and thus he sat as Shirtsleeve Smith smashed into the glade, raging like a madman.

"Elbow, yuh passed within a foot o' me—an' there was I, stuffed like a turkey! Couldn't talk, couldn't move! I aim to bust somebody's ribs. There yuh be, daggone yore hides! Whicher one manhandled me—whicher one o' yuh gents stuffed all that grass in my gullet? I got a notion to fill yuh full o' pine needles."

"Good mornin', Shirtsleeve," drawled Joe. "Hope you slep' well. How far was you aimin' to trail us last night?"

Shirtsleeve advanced, the horse-jawed countenance crimped in lines of malevolence. "How'd you know I was trailin'?"

"Always been able to smell a skunk," was Joe's deliberate answer.

"Here's where I drum a tune on yore ribs!" snorted Shirtsleeve, and stood directly over Joe.

Indigo made a noise that was indescribably contemptuous. It pricked Shirtsleeve Smith's vanity as a pin might explode a balloon. He swung toward the small partner, ready to blast him with profanity. Elbow Jim gurgled, but it was then too late. Joe's arms and hands shot out in front of him and his body sunfished through the air, striking Shirtsleeve as a battering ram. Shirtsleeve's angular frame work was too loosely coupled to absorb the impact; every joint in the man snapped, his head flew back and he bent double. Joe's fists struck Shirtsleeve's lantern face twice and the man pitched over. Elbow Jim's gun wavered uncertainly, trying to catch a clear target of Joe. Once more Indigo, who hadn't yet moved, served a useful purpose by yelling at Elbow and thus diverting the injured rustler's attention. It was, however, hardly needed. Joe—the man of leisure, the slow-talking, serene appearing man of the world—exploded like a box of dynamite. Shirtsleeve never had a chance. He was down before he understood what happened; he struggled a little and was battered again. Joe heaved him up and made a shield of him; Joe whipped the gun from the prostrate one's holster and drew a bead on Elbow.

"Drop that piece, Elbow!"

"I got orders—"

"Drop it you crazy loon or yore dead as yesterday!"

145

The summons cracked over Elbow's head, making him flinch. There he stood, a sorry and troubled figure, fighting off the deadly mists in his brain. He knew he was licked, he knew that for him the days of usefulness were over and that never again would he stand as an equal among other men. Henceforth he would be a chore boy, a half-caste creature to be pitied or laughed at or kicked about; always he would be plagued by that curtain which darkened the brightest day and cut him off from his own past, rising only for an instant—an instant in which, as now, he saw the horror of his case and the utter futility of living.

In this flickering instant of self-knowledge Elbow Jim looked on down the alley of time and found nothing there for him. There was a grain to Elbow, there was pride. Why should he, who had commanded men, now sink to the level of a camp dog? One thing he could do. He could carve his own epitaph and let men know that he was master of himself to the very end. So he turned and for a small space looked into the muzzle of Joe Breedlove's gun.

"Drop it," repeated Joe.

Elbow shrugged his shoulders and passed a glance to the still roped Indigo. He could kill Indigo, but if he did the other partner's leveled gun would crash into him before he turned his own weapon inward. And Elbow didn't wish it to be that way. Very slowly the gun in his fist veered and rose. He heard Joe Breedlove's last brittle injunction. And that was the final word that reached him from any mortal. He sent a bullet into his own tortured brain and fell.

146

"Well, by—" shouted Indigo, startled out of his calm.

Joe's revolver fell and a clucking noise passed his lips. Joe loved his fellow creatures and the sight of this moved him tremendously. "The pore devil—the pore old fella. Well, that's best." He flung up his head, hearing fresh sounds beyond the glade. The main body of rustlers were returning; that shot had warned them and it was only a matter of minutes. "Hustle over here, Indigo!"

Indigo rose and galloped toward his partner. Joe unraveled the knot holding Indigo's wrists and transferred the rope to Shirtsleeve's arms. The fellow was not entirely out but there wasn't any resistance in him. Once more he was a stuffed turkey. Indigo ran over, got the dead Elbow's gun and belt, and collected the horses.

"Them boys will think we killed Elbow," said Indigo, "which impression I hate to have 'em get. This Shirtsleeve guy ain't out of the hop enough to understand."

"Let it ride. Damn the luck, we could've had the drop on that party if they hadn't heard said shot. Now they'll watch for trouble. We've got to sift."

They swung up on horses and started through the narrow exit—the same route by which they had come. The rustlers were not in sight but the sound they made indicated an uncomfortable nearness.

"It won't do," muttered Joe. "We've got to make our own trail. Come on."

They turned, recrossed the glade and forced a way

through the brush. It was slow, nervous work; within a few minutes Annixter's booming echoes announced the discovery of what had happened. Hard on this came the leader's harsh order. "Spread an' foller. They don't get away, hear it? Knock 'em out o' the saddles! Bring down the hosses. Shouldn't of left Elbow in charge, but I didn't—Shirtsleeve, yuh yella mongrel I got a notion to ride my hoss over yuh! Come on!"

"The boy's full of business," said Joe. "Well, he can't buck this brush any faster'n we do."

"No, but he sounds powerful mean," grumbled Indigo, "and he knows this country a heap better'n us. I'm for makin' a stand on the premises."

They put the worst of the brush behind and arrived at a deer trace dodging along the uneven earth. Joe went before and jockeyed his horse into a respectable run. Overhanging boughs whipped them severely. "How about bitin' back?" persisted Indigo.

The rustlers were in full pursuit; it sounded like a stampede. "What for?" queried Joe. "All we can do is argue an' run some more. I'm awful tired of this deal. My idea is to shuffle the cards again. If we stick here we're liable to be boxed an' licked. Then when it gets dark they'll sashay the stock on over the hump—and what've we got to show for all this sulphur an' brimstone, presumin' such to happen?"

The trace dwindled to nothing, leaving them high and dry in the brush. Once again they bucked through it. The rustlers, taking advantage of the same deer trace, closed the interval. Annixter's violent shout trembled on their ears. "Mac, strike toward the draw! They're headin' for it!"

Indigo grunted. "That's advertisin' for us to stay way from said draw. Well, doggonit, this was yore bright idee in the first place. So get another idee quick or we stop an' argue. I hate to run—it blights my morals scandalous!"

The brush gave way to a more or less open stand of pines; across this they swept. Beyond was a burn with charred snags trooping side by side. On they went, the rustlers seeming to slacken the pace. "Well," decided Joe, "I hate to think of 'em gettin' away with Elkhorn's cows, knowin' what we know. Guess we better swallow some pride an' ride for help."

"Which was my recommend in the beginnin'," jeered Indigo. "It's a hell of a time to be thinkin' of it now. How d'yuh suppose we get outa this wilderness without bein' sniped at?"

The ground began to wrinkle and grow rugged. Ahead they had a vista of lava rock bereft of any kind of foliage. Acres of it, where black pinnacles reared and fell into deep pits. And beyond that at some undetermined distance the ridges dropped into the prairie. The partners had seen the bluffs descending sharply to level ground while riding across country the day before and thus they knew what lay ahead. Heat haze rested on the horizon; three hundred yards farther brought them to a draw sloping down into the prairie. Joe drew rein. He had made up his mind.

"Somebody's got to go down thataway and hit for the Elkhorn. Somebody's got to stay behind and entertain these gents a few minutes."

"That," declared Indigo with alacrity, "is my job." The wizened face flared with the only emotion it was capable of expressing, a grim and embattled plea-

149

sure; those washed blue eyes flickered, changing to an emerald green. "You travel. I'll stop 'em long enough to let yuh get a good start. Then I'll work back into the rocks an' pick my teeth."

"Pick lead from yore ears, you mean," muttered Joe. "They'll try to rub you out." His hand ripped at the buckle of his gunbelt; he flung the belt and revolver across Indigo's saddle. "You need this too."

"How about you?" protested Indigo.

"I'm runnin', not fightin'," was Joe's answer.

For an instant the partners studied each other. It was one of the few times in their joint career they had separated during trouble and it left both uneasy. Together they made a formidable, efficient machine. Asunder they were lost, like man and wife divorced. Yet there was nothing either could say at such a juncture for they were not made to say pretty sentiments. So Joe shrugged his shoulders and turned into the draw. "Be good, kid. I'll hustle back."

"Uhuh," grunted Indigo, watching his partner go. "Don't rush. I'll say I earned this fun an' they ain't no use cuttin' it short."

Joe dipped around a point of brush and was lost save for the clatter made by his pony's hoofs. And that scarce had died when Indigo flung himself into the draw and crawled up the far side. Here was a fine breastwork of rock. Back of him were other equally good shelters in case he had to retreat. He jumped from the saddle, shying his horse into an adjacent pit, and settled to his haunches.

Annixter's men raised a great noise as they came.

150

The chase had grown so hot that it made them careless for they plunged out of the concealing undergrowth and through the straggling pines with no side survey, no flanking forays. Annixter's eyes were pinned to the fugitive tracks; up to the edge of the draw they swept and halted. Annixter stood in his stirrups, looking down the draw; his arm made a semi-circular gesture and the rest of the riders closed toward him. There were six of them besides Annixter, and Indigo, raising his gun, admitted he had at last matched himself against superior odds. For Indigo that was a tremendous concession.

"One set of tracks goes down there," said Shirt-sleeve Smith, indicating the draw. "Other gent has hit for the lava rock."

"Prob'ly jus' to throw us off," snapped Annixter. "They're both foggin' for open country, you bet. Back to Elkhorn, the dam' spies. Come on. If they each help we might as well quit business."

"Don't be in no rush," sang out Indigo and placed a bullet just short of Annixter's horse. The distance made accurate revolver work out of the question, but all Indigo cared about right at present was to announce himself and keep the party occupied. The compact formation around Annixter was scattered instantly, as if a bomb had fallen in the center. Dust rose, men streamed back, spreading out. Annixter's voice rose again, though not loud enough for the entrenched Indigo to make out just what the man was saying. It didn't matter, however, for the small one's glittering green eyes saw them charge through the trees and momentarily disappear in the direction of the draw's head. That was clear enough; they meant to flank and surround him.

Indigo muttered wrathfully, "why don't they fight in the open?" and took steps to remove himself from the immediate area. The horse was no good to him out here where a yard of level ground ended in a forty yard crater or an immense monolith. Regretfully he left the pony and struck straight on toward the end of the ridge. "When a man's got to take to his own locomotion," he soliloquized, "the situation ain't bright. Anyhow, Joe's clear an' safe."

Indigo stood behind a rock shelf and watched a row of sombreros bob toward him, over on his left hand, a hundred yards away. The outlaws had deserted their horses likewise, which for a brief spell gave him the audacious idea of slipping across the draw and stealing the animals. He counted the hats and immediately decided not to be foolish; there were only five in pursuit. Evidently Annixter held a man in reserve—perhaps sent him on Joe's trail. Anyhow, it wasn't wise to buck into uncertainty. So he retreated again, keeping well out of sight. Once a burst of shots broke the silence and the lead slugs spattered an adjacent lava formation. Indigo derisively wrinkled his nose and made an insulting noise. They didn't know exactly where he was, therefore they prospected. But Indigo had cut his wisdom teeth in trouble and he wasn't to be tricked like that.

He crawled up and he slid down; he rolled over, he rested and he traveled again. The sun bit into the back of his neck and the lava rock was as sharp as broken glass. He began to sweat and at that point he

152

realized he was going to be intolerably thirsty before this day's work was ended. Right there Indigo's wrath exploded sulphurically and all the rustlers' ancestors suffered blighting comparisons. Indigo was a man who could endure all sorts of hardship and privation willingly and cheerfully, provided he did it of his own accord. But the fact was, right now, he was being driven by a collection of mangy, louse-infested, mutton-eaters and it hurt his pride to think they were the cause of all this misery. He had nearly rose up from his concealment and challenged them. Some divine angel saved Indigo from his own impulse that time, or perhaps long association with Joe Breedlove had instilled a little caution in him. He kept on. And the farther he went the narrower the ridge became. Nothing was to be seen of the rustlers. Ominous quiet held the flickering heat haze.

Twenty yards brought him to the end of his trail. He climbed the side of another huge bowl, hooked his chin over the rim and found himself staring down a matter of four hundred feet to the prairie floor. It wasn't a sheer drop, but it was abrupt enough to bar Indigo from going farther. "A centipede would shore bust his laigs goin' down that," he grunted. "Here's where we fort up."

The idea of having so much space behind him didn't suit Indigo very well. It absolutely cut off his retreat, it made this argument a last ditch affair. So he returned several yards and settled behind a pinnacle, from which he ran three small alleys. Any of them, in case of emergency, provided him with a graceful exit. The only trouble was that it left his rear open to attack. Indigo turned it over in his head and ended by going back to the very edge of the bluff. "Why do things by half? If I got to die, I got to die." With that fatalistic decision he settled himself against the most comfortable slab of lava he could find and prepared for a stormy afternoon. His pale green orbs darted across the tortured surface, seeking sign of the party, and for want of a better thing to do he emptied half a sack of cigarette tobacco in his mouth and chewed doggedly.

"Joe," he muttered, "ought to be half way to Elkhorn by now. Hope he don't take my advice too literal about not hurryin'."

Further soliloquy was abruptly terminated by the sight of a hat rising fifty yards on the right—rising and falling. Indigo fastened his attention upon it until something brushed his vision at the extreme left. Another hat. They had spread out and were sweeping the ridge top as they came. "Too thorough about it, daggone 'em," swore Indigo. He drew both guns and laid them over his parapet, grimly waiting. No more hats appeared for a little while and Indigo judged they had only been exposed to draw fire, thus identifying his location. "A barkin' dawg don't bite. Me, I ain't droppin' the hammer till I see solid flesh."

There was the faintest of sounds behind and Indigo whirled about like a tiger at bay. Down in the pit of the hollow crawled a horned toad, disturbed out of his customary somnolence. Indigo, whose nerves had been touched, cussed the toad with a roundness that would have shamed a mule skinner.

154

The toad, hearing all this reproach, skittered off. Indigo dropped his hat over the creature. "Daggone you, Oscar, what's the idee o' scarin' a gent like that? Thought somebody had clumb up behind."

The toad thumped the hat brim by way of reply. Indigo took another glance over his parapet and reached in his pocket for a piece of string. "No you don't, Oscar. Now that yuh come I reckon yuh might as well keep me company. We're goin' to see things which shore will broaden yore eddication." He slipped his hand beneath the hat and took the toad. Out came Oscar, blinking in the light, the skin beneath his throat rising and falling. Indigo threw a loop around the animal's barbed surface, laid him on the rocks and secured the string's far end beneath a loose lump of lava. Oscar was thus picketed.

"First off, Oscar," advised Indigo, "yore a livin' witness that a man can spit four hundred linear feet. It ain't a clean habit, Oscar. Wouldn't never advise yuh to chew. Wimmen don't like it. Now watch this." Indigo craned his neck over the bluff's edge and spat outward into space; for a moment he laid thus, as if waiting for an echo of the far off impact to return. Oscar walked out to the end of his tether and fell on his back, thus blinding himself to the record breaking feat. Indigo grunted. "Jus' like any other fool. Never go against the rope, Oscar."

The wizened one took another survey of the broken ground. Somebody ducked behind a hummock of lava. He heard a short signal and braced himself as five of the party popped into view and came forward on the run. Lead smashed against his parapet, splinters of rock struck his face. He took aim at the nearest and fired. The five dropped instantly. Another bullet sang above him, seeming to come from a different angle and before he had a chance to scout the area again a steady barrage played against his defense. He couldn't raise his head to see what went on, but he heard Annixter telling the rest of the rustlers to keep up the shooting and right after that he heard boots scuffing across the jagged surface. They were keeping him smothered and closing the gap.

Indigo gripped both guns in his fist and waited. "Oscar, it'll be over in a minute. This life is hell on frawgs." Reaching over he slipped the noose from the creature's neck. "You better hit for shelter." Annixter's sharp command penetrated the still air; they were not more than fifteen yards away.

156

Chapter Four

Joe swept out of the draw and across the prairie as fast as the horse would take him. He thought he heard the reverberation of pursuit down the draw, but after he got a quarter mile away from the ridge he looked back and found no one behind. That encouraged him, as well as discouraged him. His own safety was assured; Indigo's was only made the more uncertain. One thing he knew very well—the rustlers would bend every effort to capture or kill Indigo. Otherwise they were betrayed and their activities in the country were necessarily at an end.

"Should be somebody foggin' after me," he murmured to himself. "Unless they think we're both holed up in the lava. Somebody must've seen my tracks headin' down the draw."

But there was nobody behind, not even as the bluffs grew dim behind the haze and at that point he decided the rustlers had figured his tracks to be only a blind. It was queer, too, they couldn't spot him out in the level ground from their vantage point. It must be they had their heads pretty close to the lava. The thought made him grin wryly. "Indigo'll see they don't stand very high in the air."

After that he discarded these speculations and took to nursing speed out of the pony. About forty-five minutes later he stopped the lathered, exhausted animal in front of the Elkhorn porch and dropped out of the saddle.

Stovall was in his accustomed chair. He saw the girl Julie hurrying through the house toward the door. And before he could say anything the young foreman, Slip, popped around the corner at a run. "What's up?" he demanded.

Stovall motioned the foreman to be silent, the ruddy face turning a deeper red. "Slip, ain't you learned politeness yet? Dammit, a man'd think you was a pilgrim in the country. Julie—Julie!"

"Yes, dad." The girl was framed in the doorway, looking curiously at Joe. The silver-haired puncher removed his hat and ducked his head.

"Get the man a drink. Step to the porch, sir, an' take a seat. It's another hot day."

"Why, I'd reckon it was," agreed Joe. Time pressed, but he was an old hand and he recognized Stovall's ingrained courtesy. The West changed and grew away from men like the Elkhorn owner; folks put less faith in the ancient etiquette, but Stovall kept to it while the youthful foreman simmered and looked dourly on. The girl returned with a brimming dipper and a flashing smile. Joe drank.

"I'll be thankin' you, ma'am," said he, returning the dipper. The foreman stirred angrily as he watched the two of them stand so near together and

158

for the moment so oblivious to all other things.

"Yore horse needs rest," suggested Stovall, "better lay over."

Joe heard in this an invitation to speak his piece. So he came directly to the issue, talking in slow, clipped words. "My partner and I was ridin' south yesterday. I guess you understand that we been trained to mind our own business, no matter what happens."

"Knew it when I saw you," interrupted Stovall. "Know a old hand when I see one. About gone from the country now."

"What's all this parley about?" grunted Slip.

Joe proceeded as if he hadn't heard the young foreman. "Accidental, the other night we struck a party that mistook us for somebody else. They spilled the beans. A matter of rustlin' some cows. I'll just say that we knew yore stock was to be rustled. We knew it when we came past yore place."

The young foreman pointed an accusing finger. "Then why didn't you say something? That's a pretty kind of talk to spill now!"

Joe was looking at Stovall, almost apologetically. "I was hopin' you'd ketch on to my last remark. We been taught to mind our own business strictly."

Stovall's ruddy face lost some of its color and the coal black eyes snapped. Julie had retreated to the doorway and had her attention riveted on Joe. "I was raised in the same school myself," said Stovall, quietly. "I've seen men killed for not keepin' out o' what wasn't their affair. You got nothin' to be sorry about."

"Well," went on Joe, still more apologetically, "when my partner an' I rode away from here we—well, we figgered it wasn't exactly right. So, not bein' able to squeal, an' yet knowin' what we did know, we decided to go back an' see the thing through. Aim was to throw in with the rustler gents an' later run yore stuff back on the range without sayin' anything to anybody. Point is, we was mistook by said parties for a couple northern rustlers who was to take yore stock an' fog it over the line. That's how we could swing the deal without a fight, or without blabbin'."

"Go ahead," said Stovall, with hardly any emotion in his words.

Joe turned to the girl. She nodded imperceptibly and seemed to withdraw still farther into the house. "It didn't work out," finished Joe. "Trouble. Real rustlers from the north turned up. My partner is barricaded up in the lava an' yore critters are hid somewhere along the pass. That's why I'm here. If it was only a matter of me an' Indigo I wouldn't bother you folks. But you stand to lose some cows."

The young foreman erupted disbelief. "I didn't like the way you fellows drifted in the last time. Didn't believe what you said. Don't believe it now. Sounds to me like yo're a couple of highbinders that got pinched an' now you're yelpin' for help. All this high an' mighty talk about not wantin' to squeal—"

Julie spoke for the first time. "Slip, stop that."

The foreman threw up his flushed face and stared at her in astonishment. "Listen, Julie, I'm responsible for this ranch and I can't go swallowin' a lot of honky—"

"Be quiet, Slip," said she.

"Is it his word over mine, then?" cried Slip.

"Don't you know an honest man by sight, Slip?" she asked him. And when Joe turned to watch her she was gone from the doorway.

Stovall's hands plucked at his blanket, and if ever a man struggled with a desire it was the Elkhorn owner. There was something so passionately wistful in the old man's face that Joe dropped his head. Stovall gave his foreman abrupt orders. "Call out the crew. Saddle this gentleman another horse."

"To ram ourself into hot lead an' a trap?" asked Slip.

"Do as I say, Slip. Hustle it."

The foreman retreated, calling to the crew. Joe rolled a cigarette, still feeling the necessity of an apology. "Reckon we made a mess of it all around. Either should of stayed out altogether or went in altogether."

"It reminds me—" began Stovall. He never finished that sentence, seeming to be lost in his past. A little later a slow grin spread over his ruddy features. "Hell of a way for a ranchman to take bad news, ain't it? You'd think I ought to be sore. But it's been so long since I saw anybody gallop up on a lathered brute that it sorter takes me back. Can you lick 'em with my boys?"

"I reckon," was Joe's brief answer.

"I'd give every red cent I own to go along," said Stovall, and the grin disappeared. "I don't believe you give me a name, cowboy."

"Joe Breedlove," said the tall one. "Happens to be my true name."

161

"Any name would've done," was Stovall's quick response. "Well, Whitey, you and yore partner have got a job here any time. Think it over."

The foreman rode around the house with a quartette of Elkhorn men behind him and an extra pony. Joe climbed up, nodding at the surly Slip. Stovall's black eyes held a glitter as he gave his last order to the youth. "Now, yo're takin' instructions from Whitey on this party. What he says goes. Hear it?"

"You're the boss," grunted Slip.

"You bet," snorted Stovall. "Ride!"

Joe swung away. Just as he reached the crest of a small ridge he turned to catch another look of the Elkhorn house. Stovall gripped the arms of his chair, trying to rise; and beside him was the girl, her hand above her eyes. It rose to him, and fell. The youthful foreman caught that gesture and he pushed his mount alongside Joe's angrily. "Who the hell are you, anyhow, to come here an' mislead folks? I'll play this game, fella, but you bet I'm protectin' the Stovalls. Leave yore betters alone."

Joe shook his head. "I know jus' how you feel, Slip," said he, gently. "I had a girl, too, when I was yore age."

"Keep her off yore tongue!" snapped the young foreman. "An' if yo're any man a-tall, don't play ducks an' drakes with a good family."

Joe held his peace. The young fellow was all right, he was doing the best he could and he didn't really mean to pass the boundary of politeness. An older head might have understood, but Slip was very

162

young and he felt his responsibilities. So Joe made the proper allowances, sympathizing with the man, yet all the while remembering Julie Stovall's gray eyes, and the smile she had given him. "It'd be a dreary world without a woman," he murmured to himself. "Wonder what Indigo'd think about workin' on the Elkhorn?"

"What was that?" asked the foreman.

"Bear a little left," said Joe.

Nothing more was said for a half-hour. The ridge stood clearer through the haze and the sheer bluffs at the western extremity began to show their ochre and black coloring. Joe followed the trail he had made earlier, a trail that led them directly toward the draw. A mile or two from the draw's entrance he began to debate the advisability of circling and entering the rugged land by the timbered half. He dismissed the move as a time waster. If Annixter's bunch were on the lookout they would see this party crossing the open land and prepare accordingly. Best to strike up the draw and take what came. He announced this decision to young Slip. The foreman, stirred by the proximity of a pitched battle, forgot his resentment and his suspicions.

"Where's yore partner?"

"Corraled somewhere in the lava."

"It's been near two hours, ain't it?" wondered young Slip. "Which is a pretty long time for one man to stand off five-six. Say, what gang is this? You ain't told me yet."

"Annixter's."

"The hell! Say, yore partner's out of luck by this time."

163

Joe turned on Slip with a swift, brittle retort. "They don't grow Indigo's kind down here, my boy. Don't feel bereaved none till you see him dead."

"Well, what's the play to be?"

"Bust into 'em when we see the color of their whiskers. Look sharp. Spread out a little. If there's any dickerin', I'll do it. But don't go to sleep in the saddle meanwhile. Pick a man an' keep yore eyes on him. Up we go."

They reached the draw's mouth and threaded its tortuous course. It narrowed and grew steep; rocks went clattering down the slope behind. Somewhere was a single shot followed by silence. "Hustle it!" snapped Joe. "They ain't had sense enough to quit foolin' with Indigo yet."

The draw swooped along a final sharp grade and brought them to the exact point the partners had parted earlier in the day. Joe dropped to the ground and ran up to where he commanded a view of the lava bed. Another shot blasted the sultry stillness.

"They're givin' it up. Comin' back. Ain't seen us yet. Spread along the ground. Wait till I give the word!" whispered Joe.

The Elkhorn punchers flung themselves against the earth at wide intervals. Joe plastered himself at the draw's rim, peering between boulders. Annixter's men came back, threading the lava pits, ducking in and out of view. There were five of them and Joe, casting up the account, wondered what had happened to the other one. Back watching the rustled stock, or dead by Indigo's gun. Well, it would soon be

164

discovered. Another shot cracked across the barren strip and Annixter's men sank momentarily down, turning away from the hidden Elkhorn party. Joe's heart swelled a little and he felt like shouting; for Indigo's warped and wiry figure popped out of a depression seventy yards beyond the rustlers and waved his gun in a plain invitation for them to return and fight. It was beyond any decent gun range but the rustlers opened fire. Indigo waggled his thumb and fingers in a ribald manner; his yell split the air. Then he sank back. The rustlers took up the retreat once more. Annixter's heavy voice rose blasphemously, no more than fifty feet distant. Joe waited another dragging minute, feet doubling beneath him. His Stetson bobbed toward the Elkhorn boys. Together they sprang up and faced Annixter's crew.

"Up with 'em!" snapped Joe. "No parley! Up with the flippers! First man moves is first man dead!"

The rustlers stopped in their tracks, completely taken off guard. Annixter's russet beard flamed in the sun, his body weaved forward and back as if he gathered momentum for the draw. For the rest of the party surrender came quickly. One by one hands rose. But Annixter looked directly at Joe Breedlove, weighing the silver-haired partner with a long, harsh glance. The power of it was like a rifle bullet and when he spoke, arms still at his sides, the somber, scornful words augured the danger in him.

"Thought you was back there behind the rocks, hombre. I ain't givin' in easy. Make it a fair deal. Drop yore gun an' we'll hit for the draw."

Joe shook his head. "I cut my wisdoms long time ago, Annixter. Why should I swap shots now? Ain't after yore hide. Up with the flippers."

"Yuh rat! They ain't nothin' lowerin' a sneakin' spy like you. Somebody'll tear the liver out o' yore ribs one o' these fine days. And it'll be Bo Annixter. Mind that."

"Up with the flippers," droned Joe.

Annixter gave in. The Elkhorn boys moved on, disarmed the trapped ones, and herded them into the draw. Joe circled Annixter before lifting the rustler's gun; then his arms felt along the man's ribs. "Stinger's drawn, Slip. Take him away."

Indigo came across the lava casually, a cigarette drooping in his lips. And from the disillusion on his face, the weary carriage of his shoulders and the expressionless cast of his washed blue eyes he seemed to tell the disordered universe that it was just another bad day.

"Well, Joe."

"Well, Indigo."

"Back again, uh? Must've hurried."

"Oh, so-so. Any trouble."

"Not much. They rushed me. One of 'em out there. Not defunct, but harmless." Then a small gleam of interest came to the dyspeptic countenance. "Say, I spit four hundred feet. Tie that."

Joe grinned. "Didn't think it was that far down the bluff side."

"Hell," grunted Indigo, "I thought mebbe you'd bite. Reckon I'll spend the rest o' my life tryin' to convince folks. Well, what next?"

The partners returned to the bluff's rim and picked

up the wounded rustler. It was Shirtsleeve Smith and the man was in poor shape. They lugged him back to the draw where the Elkhorn bunch had tied the prisoners into the saddles. Shirtsleeves was likewise lashed; they were ready for the trip home.

"Listen," growled Annixter to the Elkhorn foreman. "I didn't know yuh had these fellas on yore payroll."

"They ain't," explained Slip. "Strangers to me."

Annixter exploded in Joe's face. "Why, yuh damn' crooks! So yuh was jus' stealin' from me, huh? Wanted to let us get the blame for rustlin' while you piked off with 'em!"

"What's that?" asked the youthful foreman, growing suspicious again.

"A couple of sagebrush tinhorns!" snorted Annixter. "Without guts enough to steal their own cows so they double-cross me! Listen, you two. I'll live to tear yore livers out! Mind that—an' I'll see yuh roast in hell for killin' pore old Elbow—"

The youthful foreman dropped his head; the next moment both partners were covered with the Elkhorn guns. Slip's countenance blazed with suspicion. "It's what I thought all the time. Your scheme didn't work an' yuh got in a jackpot, so yuh crawls to the old man for help. I thought so. Stretch 'em elbows."

Indigo was on the verge of an explosion. Joe stilled him with a soft word and met the irate Slip's glance. "Son," he murmured, "is that all you've got in yore head?" The mildness and the serenity of a summer's morning rested upon the tall one's face. At the moment he seemed as if he were giving the young foreman fatherly advice; the hazel eyes beamed gently.

"Keep yore dirty tongue off—" began Slip, and checked himself. "Put up yore hands."

Indigo exploded. "What's yore itch, yuh bottle-fed crib sucker?"

"You'll itch in jail," retorted Slip. "Hands up. You'll never dirty Elkhorn again."

Indigo looked to Joe, the tall partner nodded back, raising his arms. "All right. It won't be long." He smiled at Slip. "Human nature is a big book. Read it sometime. We won't be in the lockup more'n two hours. Let's go."

Slip turned to Annixter. "Where's the critters?"

"Find 'em," muttered Annixter. "Well—north o' the pass. Elbow's down that trail, too. Take care o' him."

Slip nodded to one of his men. "That's yore job." The rest of the riders gathered behind the prisoners and pushed them down the draw. At dusk they reached town. The sheriff put Annixter's bunch in one cell and the partners in another. The Elkhorn men went home.

"Yore prediction," said Indigo, three hours later, "is no good. Here's the finish o' a good impulse. Next time yuh desire to help anybody, strangle the idee. Stomp on it. Ain't yuh discovered yet they's nothin' meaner in this world than human nature?"

Joe rolled a cigarette. It was dark in the cell and a brooding silence pervaded the jail. Through the barred window they saw the yellow lamplight twinkling out of a saloon opposite; boots scraped across the town walk and soft speech floated upward. Joe's match wavered in the gloom and went out, but by the moment's illumination Indigo saw his partner smiling. "Some people is bad, some is good," he murmured. "But most of us is half an' half, which makes life interestin'. Annixter, now, is all bad—or as near to it as anybody could get. The young foreman fella is fifty-fifty. He's got a good heart an' sound impulses but he lets his temper get the best o' him. As for the—"

"Yeah," jeered Indigo, "go ahead an' tell me somebody all to the good."

"The girl," said Joe, just above a whisper.

Indigo moved uneasily. "Well, I think we're the singed ducks, m'self. That sheriff, they say, is desirous o' makin' a record."

"Won't be very long now," drawled Joe.

"What makes yuh so all-fired certain?" asked Indigo.

"I know. Say, how would you like to hire out again?"

Indigo was silent for a long spell. He knew what was coming, he had seen the portents in the sky some time before. It dragged in his spirits, made him weary and depressed. "Who to?"

Joe's answer was too casual. "Oh, we got an invite to work for Elkhorn. Seems to me maybe we've done drifted plenty long. Don't it strike you like that, Indigo?"

Indigo merely grunted. Joe squinted through the darkness and found his partner humped over on the bunk's edge.

169

Boots shuffled up the stairway and a key scraped the lock. The Sheriff issued a reluctant invitation. "Come on out, you buzzards. The Elkhorn got soft-hearted an' they ain't makin' no charges. Personal, I'd like to see you get justice."

"Justice," drawled Joe, rising, "has many meanin's, sher'ff. Which meanin' was you alludin' to?"

The sheriff grunted. Indigo and Joe passed down the stairs to the office and found Slip, the young foreman, waiting for them. He had his hat off and the light glimmered along his curly hair. He was a good looking youngster, Joe decided. And at present he met Joe's eyes with a straight, frank glance. "Listen," said he, "I guess I got off on the wrong foot. Got the hell bawled out of me by the old man an' Julie. That's why I'm back. Mebbe you're off me permanent, but I jus' want you to know that I'd cut off my hands for Elkhorn an' the folks on it. Give 'em their guns, Sher'ff."

Joe was smiling, the sweet and twisted smile that was so much a part of him. He put out his hand. "I was young once, Slip," he murmured. "Don't I know how it feels? Once I had a girl—"

"I'm out of it I reckon," interrupted young Slip, gruffly. His eyes dropped as if to conceal some betraying emotion. When he raised his head again he had set his face as tight as he could. "They want you to come back. The old man—and Julie. Let's go outside."

The partners crossed the threshold. There was a rig standing in front of the jail and Julie Stovall sat in

170

the driver's seat, waiting. Her face was in the shadows and Joe couldn't see her eyes, but her words tinkled across the interval like the notes of a flute. "We're sorry. All of us. So is Slip. Slip has always fought so hard for us. We want you to come back. I—I hope you will."

"I'll go get the hosses," muttered Indigo, and went away. He stumbled on a plank and swore bitterly. And at the stable he saddled both horses in a kind of blind fury. The stableman started to talk. Indigo flared up. "Shut yore mouth, yuh galoot!" Out he rode, leading Joe's pony. "I can see the end right now," he grunted.

He arrived at the buggy. Joe mounted and the three men followed the rig out of town and along the road to the Elkhorn. There was a soft breeze bringing up the aroma of the desert and the moon hung on the horizon like a Hallowe'en lantern. The lights of town faded, the horses' hoofs made a lulling rhythm on the hardpacked road. Joe touched his partner's arm—a rare thing for him. "It's all right with you, Indigo?"

"I reckon," grunted Indigo and said no more. They crossed a creek and ran onward through the night. Slip, the foreman, muttered something and spurred ahead of the party. They wheeled around an area of boulders and took a short climb. Of a sudden Indigo took up the slack in his reins and halted. "I forgot somethin' in town, Joe. You go on. See yuh later."

"What—" began Joe, likewise stopping. But Indigo never answered. He was fifty feet away, traveling like a crazy man.

171

"It's the end," muttered Indigo, looking up to the black sky. "Yeah. Fare-you-well to old times. Joe's got a girl an' Indigo rides alone from now on. Hell!"

He was not an imaginative man, this warped and pessimistic and morose rider of the range; he was not one to nourish regrets for a lost past, he seldom ever found himself lifted in anticipation for the future. But tonight marked a milestone in his life, tonight was the forking of one more trail and down one of those trails he had to ride alone. Ride alone on into the southern horizon. All roads had an ending, all men came to the great divide and crossed into the misty land. Well, that didn't matter. But it would be lonely without Joe. How many a mile had they traversed, side by side? How many a campfire had they built together, how many a fight had they seen to a good ending? They were partners who knew each other so well that they understood the twist of each gesture, the inflection of each syllable.

"Why should I stick on the ranch an' see him slip into double harness?" he muttered fiercely. "The time had to come, sooner or later, but why should I hang around an' see him swap to another partner?"

The lights of town blinked across the land. Indigo shook his head. "I ain't shore about Joe an' that girl. Well, I know what she sees in him. Any woman ought to be proud o' Joe. Lots of 'em have looked twice an' wished. Yeah. But Joe's thirty-five an' she's no more'n twenty. When he's fifty she's thirty-five. Well? I ain't shore Joe'll like double rig an' a fenced pasture. Slip now, is her age. They're a matched pair."

Indigo was a realist. And he knew that save for

Joe's arrival Julie Stovall would probably have married Slip. Things happened that way. And they were a matched pair. What she saw in Joe Breedlove was the same thing other women and men saw in the silver-haired one. Joe brought a touch of mystery with him and a touch of romance. He was handsome and when he smiled the love of life sprang across his face, to weld others to him.

"Yeah, she'd married Slip. Slip's young an' still flighty. But he's got the makin's of a good fella. She owns him, an' she knows it. Didn't I see her look at him once? They'd make a matched team. I ain't shore about her an' Joe. By God, why has things got to be thataway? It ain't a fair swap. Joe's got a long trail behind an' they was another girl way back."

On the edge of town he made one more observation. "If she lost him she'd get over it."

He dropped the reins over a hitching rack and wandered into the saloon. The lights blinded his eyes and he blinked around at the scattering crowd, the washed blue orbs plainly hostile, plainly threatening. At the counter he raised his fingers to the barkeep. The barkeep slid a bottle and glass toward Indigo, saying:

"It's a fine night, partner."

"The hell it is," snapped Indigo. He took the bottle and glass to a corner table and sat down. For some time he looked into the amber liquid as if seeing a great many pictures there. Then he poured, raised the glass and saluted the wall. "Here's to yuh, kid. Won't see yore kind again. Indigo rides solitaire from now on."

The trail ahead would be across the same old desolate prairie, the night fire would be by the same barren pines. And somewhere beyond the heat haze there would be an end. "Me," muttered Indigo, "I'm goin' to get so drunk tonight a hog wouldn't sleep in the same bed. Good bye, kid."

He drank. He drank again. Chips clattered at an adjacent table. Somebody called to him, inviting him to take a hand. Indigo half turned and the frigid blue eyes devastated the players. "Mind yore own business," grunted Indigo, and poured himself another glass.

He had his back to the door and therefore didn't see a tall man sweep through and in. Didn't see him sweep the room and then walk toward the corner. But he heard a familiar voice call his name roughly and before he could look up he saw a bronzed fist flash across the table and knock bottle and glass to the floor. Joe Breedlove towered over him; all the humor and all the serenity was gone and in its stead was a tight, bleak bitterness. Joe looked shockingly old and tired.

"What the hell are yuh doin' here?" he demanded. "Guzzlin' like an' old soak. Get up. We're ridin'."

"Where?"

"South," muttered Joe. "Come on."

They went out, with the crowd watching, and they climbed up to the saddles and turned through the street, heading south, away from town, away from Elkhorn. Taking up the pilgrimage that had been interrupted the last few days. And some time later in the night when the lights no longer winked at them

174

and the stark shadows wrapped around them, Joe spoke.

"It jus' wouldn't stick, Indigo. I ain't her kind. By God, I ain't! If ever she thought so, she'll change her mind later when she marries Slip."

Indigo was shrewd. He held his tongue. And if he had spoken, the thing he had on his mind would have seemed so completely foreign to his nature that Joe Breedlove would never have believed it. But Indigo, looking up to the stars, found the world good.

BLOCKBUSTER FICTION FROM PINNACLE BOOKS!